LYKOI LARCENY

CHAPTER ONE

Marjorie Hardaway ducked her head as she walked into the community centre, avoiding the low hanging string of tinsel across the doorway. "Do you need me to hold the ladder?" she asked the scowling teenage boy who was fixing it to the wall. "You don't seem very steady."

She grabbed hold of the base of the stepladder, though the boy had responded to her offer with stony silence. With three clicks of a staple gun, he turned and dismounted, jumping from the third step up to avoid her hands.

"I'm fine. It's only a metre high." He slouched over to a cardboard box and pulled another string of tinsel out, this one tangled around a set of Christmas lights.

"Careful," Allie Wilson said, emerging from the back room. "If you jerk those too hard, you're sure to break a bulb and then you'll have to locate it in the row of fifty identical lights."

"I don't know why you can't just buy new packets," the boy grumbled even as he obeyed and unpicked the tangle with more care. "They're only a few bucks down at the Christmas warehouse."

"It must be nice to be made of money," Allie said, rolling her eyes at Marjorie. "But unless you're picking up the tab, we'll make do with last year's."

Marjorie hid a smile as the teenage boy muttered under his breath. "I've dropped by to pick up the approximate numbers for the Christmas party. Esme said you'd have the final tally."

"Well, as final as it gets with this sort of

thing," Allie said, curling her finger for Marjorie to follow and heading out the door. "There'll always be extra turning up on the day when they discover there's a lot more to entertaining young ones than letting them watch the telly. Likewise, confirmed attendees will wake up at noon, forgetting there's anything special on at all."

"A guesstimate is fine with me." Marjorie tucked the note into her pocket and peered around the door as the teenager began his jerky ascent of the stepladder once again. "Should he be doing that?"

Allie snorted. "I'm just glad to find Jon Roscoe working at anything. The first few days of his community service, the kid wouldn't lift a finger. It wasn't until I threatened not to sign off on his hours that he finally came around."

"Perhaps it's the magic of Christmas." Marjorie twiddled her fingers, imagining sparkles. "He's found the spirit of giving."

"He's found the spirit of his free time jeopardised, more like." Allie put a hand on her hip and sighed. "I've always been happy to assist with the young offender's program and I'd rather they were in here, helping out, than on the streets or in a jail cell, but honestly?" She shook her head. "It gets harder every year."

Marjorie was about to dismiss the sentiment as the same nonsense complaint she uttered every couple of weeks when her mood was low, then saw the tiredness etched in the older woman's face. Allie was always so full of positivity and warmth, she usually appeared young. Right now she looked every one of her sixty-seven years.

"Hey now. If you need some help, I can order the lad about for a bit," Marjorie said, giving the woman a firm hug. "He can't be any worse at listening to me than my kittens are."

Allie sniffed away a tear and shook her head again, this time accompanied by the hint of a smile. "No, you're alright. I'm just letting everything get to me lately. And the lad's not so bad. He coated over some graffiti on the front wall that stood six feet tall. I'd never have been able to do all that."

"Who would tag the community hall?" Marjorie's voice shot up the register with indignation.

"A father who thinks because we host the foster kids' Christmas party, we're the ones responsible for him losing custody of his son. I called the police down here and they seemed to know who it was, so hopefully, they'll get it sorted."

"I guess it's a hard time of year for some people." Marjorie tried to imagine her kittens being taken away and having none of them to share the festive days ahead. Awful. And even as a crazy cat lady, she had to admit it would be nothing as bad as being separated from your child.

Allie cleared her throat and tsked as Jon leaned to the left, rocking the legs of the stepladder. "Sometimes I think this is a younger woman's game."

"Hardly." Marjorie glanced at Allie's tight grey curls and neat outfit, then stared in dismay at her own fur-covered jeans and shirt. "Anyone younger would either mother him or let him walk all over her. What they need is an old lady with an iron rod for a spine who doesn't put up with any of their feeble excuses."

The older woman snorted. "Iron lady, am I?"

Marjorie was about to answer when Jon poked his head into the room. "I've hung the tinsel. What's next?"

"Untangle the lights and make sure they work," Allie said promptly. "And feel free to refer to the list I gave you this morning if you need a reminder."

The young man walked away, and Marjorie coloured to think he might have overheard their conversation. "How long is he here for?"

"Six weeks, so that'll take us up to the end of January. Once he gets through the Christmas rush, though, there won't be nearly as much work."

"I can't imagine he'll complain about that."

But Allie's expression changed to one of concern. "Idle hands…"

"The library is always asking for volunteers to read during story time. If you need a break, send him over to Glynis and let her deal with him for a few hours." At the thought of the horror that would cross the stern librarian's face if Jon appeared, slouching and scowling, Marjorie giggled. "And you never know, he might enjoy it."

A loud honk from a van interrupted their conversation and the two women hurried outside to see what had prompted the toot.

"I've got a load of pressies for you," Felix Corwin called out, giving them both a wide smile.

"For the kids, you mean," a disgruntled voice said from the side door. When Marjorie followed the sound, she found Dotty Woodrow standing in front of a huge stack of gifts, all unwrapped.

"Oh, my goodness. The community's been so generous!" Marjorie stared in wonder at the different toys on offer. The model trains, planes, and automobiles she remembered from her childhood had been massively upgraded with remote controls and powerful engines. No pushing a matchbox-sized tin car around a plastic track for the new generation.

A man appeared out of the depths of the van, giving her a start. Then she saw it was Braden with an amused grin that showed he knew full well his sudden appearance had given her heart an extra thump.

"Are you staying around to help us wrap these up?" Braden asked, jumping down into the carpark and dusting the front of his trousers. "Felix and I will do our best but... You know... Clumsy male fingers."

"Amazing how you can rewire second-hand electronics and get them working as good as new, but you can't apply sticky tape to paper." Marjorie smiled. "One could almost be misled into thinking it's a lame excuse to get out of work."

"How many did we lose?" Allie said, ignoring the men and talking directly to Dotty.

"Only a dozen or so. We've got some we had to unwrap after the donators painstakingly gift-wrapped them for us but a few on the route baulked at that and kept the presents. The rest were wrapping-paper free already."

"Why are you unwrapping them if you've just got to wrap them up again?" Marjorie asked in astonishment. "It seems like a lot of extra work."

"It is, which is why we ask for any donations to come as is," Allie said, pinching her nose. "But not everyone follows instructions."

"We have to see what the gift is," Dotty explained further. "If we don't know what's inside, there could be a disaster on Christmas when we're handing them out."

Braden gasped and held his palm against his chest. "You mean, someone might get the wrong Barbie?"

"Someone might get a box without a doll in it at all," Dotty said with her mouth pressed in a thin line. "We didn't come up with the policy for fun. Some members of our community have a twisted idea of pranks."

"Who would prank a child?" Marjorie was overcome with horror. "Especially a foster kid who's already having a rough time."

"You'd be surprised," Dotty muttered darkly before Allie clapped her hands together.

"How about we move the conversation onto a more pleasant topic?" she said, smiling at the group. "Braden, did you repair all the donations?"

For the past year, he'd been accepting gifts of broken electronics with the sole focus of repairing them to an 'as new' state for Christmas. Game consoles could stay at the community centre for use by anybody dropping in, while others would be sold via online auction to raise money for the following year's event.

"A few were determined to stay broken," Braden admitted with a sheepish grin. "But we've got a half dozen consoles in working order for the games room and bids are coming in thick and fast for the rest."

"Excellent." Allie gave him a quick hug that had Braden blushing. "It'll be great for the teens to come and play here when things are rough at home."

"Not just the teens," Braden said with a cheeky grin. "I've been thinking of arranging a competition for people of any age to join. It's a sport, you know."

"Of course, it is," Marjorie said, trying not to giggle as Dotty gave an exaggerated eye-roll.

"I'd better get this truck back home," Felix said, making an exaggerated show of checking his watch. "If there're any more donations that get called in from now until the party, tell them I'll pick them up on Christmas Eve."

"Not so fast." Allie stepped between him and the van door. "Thank you for collecting the presents but they still need to be wrapped and labelled."

"But I—"

"You volunteered for the whole shebang,

not just the fun bits. Now get on in there, or I'll have Dotty drag you by the ears!"

Felix took a few dragging steps towards the community centre entrance, then slyly slipped a hand around Braden's wrist as he too tried to sidle away. "Not so fast. You heard the lady."

Allie shook her head as Dotty herded the men inside. "Between them and young Jon, I think I'd rather supervise a young offender any day."

"I can stay if you want the extra help," Marjorie offered. "The kittens have an hour until they expect feeding and I can put the rest of my chores off until tomorrow."

"Not if one of those tasks is getting the ingredients you need for the Christmas day baking. Won't the wholesale warehouse be a madhouse the closer it gets to the big day?"

Marjorie had to agree. "Everything will be. I don't understand why two days' holiday cause so much havoc. When I was growing up, every shop shut for the weekend and nobody was panicked into mass buying goods."

"We appear to have lost the art of planning ahead." Allie jerked around as a crash sounded from inside the centre. "I'd better get back to it."

Marjorie made a commiserating noise, but Allie had already rushed indoors, out of sight. The fresh paint on the side of the building caught the afternoon sun and reflected it back, turning the car park gravel yellow. If she squinted, a message was still visible, a faint shade darker than the covering paint. It would need another coat before the job was done, but she supposed Jon needed to wait until the first layer dried.

"Whatever happened to the Christmas spirit?" she said under her breath while walking back to her car. With volunteers ensuring the less fortunate members of the community received a hearty Christmas meal and presents, there should have been happiness and excitement in the air. Instead, everyone was frayed around the edges.

Putting the dismal thoughts aside, Marjorie headed back to her café. Although it was already past five o'clock, she groaned to see the builders were still dotted about the section in front of hers.

They were laying the foundations for the next-door building, with the actual construction to take place next year. Although she was glad to see progress being made, the raucous language hurled about made her uneasy for her customers. The sooner they were gone, the better.

"This one of yours?" a man called out as Marjorie fumbled with the keys to the entrance. "He looks in a bad way."

She rushed over, hearing a piteous mew from underneath a tarpaulin covering up a sheaf of metal rods. "Here, kitty."

"Ugly thing," the man said, sniffing and wiping his nose on the back of his arm. "It looked half dead."

"If you were half dead, I'm sure you'd look ugly too," Marjorie snapped, lifting the edge of the cover and spying reflective grey eyes.

"You want a hand with that?" The man stepped forward and yanked the entire sheet off the pile, exposing a tiny kitten to the sunlight and setting the rods clanging against each other. "What a sight, eh?"

"Come on," Marjorie said, clicking her tongue in encouragement as the kitten eyed her warily. "Wouldn't you like something to eat?"

"I've got a bit of sandwich leftover from lunch if you want to try that."

But it wasn't needed. The kitten pounced on Marjorie's outstretched hand and rubbed along her arm, before running into the shelter of her crouching legs. "Hey, now. It's okay. I've got you." She picked up the small cat, cradling it against her chest.

"Where's it hurt?" the builder asked, pointing at the sticky crimson smudge the kitten had left on Marjorie's arm. "You need a lift to the vet?"

She stared at the smudge, turning so it was in full sunlight.

Blood.

CHAPTER TWO

Marjorie gave a shiver and closed her eyes, willing her stomach contents to stay put. She turned to the builder, accepting his offer to drive with gratitude as her head became giddy. "The closest vet is on Jollies Pass Road. Do you know where that is?"

"Sure do," he said, opening the car door while she struggled inside with her new charge. "We've got accommodation along the same road."

The man kept up a constant stream of chatter during the short journey, informing

Marjorie of his name, occupation, family, and money woes—Barney Baxter, builder, wife and one son, and never enough, was there?

Although she only listened with one ear, Marjorie was grateful for the one-sided conversation. The kitten cradled in her lap had trembled from the moment the car started, and she was too squeamish to search for obvious signs of injury herself. All she could do was hope and pray.

"Emergency," she called out, entering Kitcare Veterinary Services at a trot, Barney close on her heels. "We've got an injured kitten."

The receptionist hurried out the back and soon the vet—Walter Argyle—emerged with a worried expression on his face. Marjorie thrust the small cat into his arms and stepped back, wringing her hands.

"Did he get hit by a car?"

"I don't know," she said, glancing at Barney who also shook his head. "We just found him like that. Will—?" she broke off as her throat clutched and waited a few seconds before trying again. "Will he be okay?"

"I'll take him into the office and get him cleaned up enough to see the damage and we can work from there." Walter left the room and Marjorie collapsed into a chair, her shoulders shaking.

"Are you alright if I head off now?"

She jerked back in surprise, staring at Barney through wide eyes. "But you're staying, aren't you? I don't have my car."

"It's knocking off time." The builder made a big show of checking his watch. "Or ten minutes past, already."

Marjorie bit back on a retort about how, if she'd known, she'd have taken her own vehicle. It wasn't true because even in the chair she felt lightheaded. Even so, it was the principle of the thing.

"Can't you make this your good deed for Christmas?" Marjorie patted her pockets, feeling the keys to the café and her phone but no bulge to indicate her wallet. She'd probably left it upstairs at home since she'd only been popping into town to check in at the community centre. That ruled out a taxi and Hanmer Springs hadn't quite got the hang of Uber just yet.

It left her with shanks pony, then.

Barney hadn't answered so Marjorie shrugged. "If you need to be somewhere else, don't let me stop you."

As the builder cheerfully waved goodbye Marjorie didn't know if she felt more miffed at herself for saying something so passive-aggressive or for it not having any effect. She crossed her arms and the tackiness on them was a grim reminder of the blood on the kitten.

"Can I use your bathroom to clean up?" When the reception nodded and pointed to the door, Marjorie gave a sigh of relief. The paper towels for drying hands weren't the best at cleaning dried blood off skin, but they did a good enough job for her stomach to stop complaining.

"Nothing wrong with him," Walter

announced as Marjorie came back into the waiting room. "Come on through."

"Why was he bleeding, then?"

"Oh, it's blood, but it doesn't belong to this little fellow." The vet chuckled as the kitten launched himself across the table and into Marjorie's lap. "Looks like you're someone's new favourite."

"So, he isn't hurt at all?"

"With his scant fur covering, he shouldn't be outside, so he might be cold. From now on, he needs to be strictly an indoor cat. But as for physical harm, I couldn't find even a cut or scratch. Just as well, too. That's one expensive kitty."

"This one?" Marjorie gave it a side-eye, trying to work out the breed. The kitten had sparse fur but not bare enough to be a Sphynx or a Devon Rex. His big grey eyes studied her as closely as she studied him, appearing close to human.

"He's a Lykoi and I know exactly where he belongs." Walter fiddled with an old Filo-fax until giving a cry of triumph. "No wonder he ended up at your house. His owner only lives a couple of blocks away."

Now it was Walter's turn to get Marjorie's side-eye. In Hanmer, a block could mean anything from a half dozen houses to an acre. "Who is it?"

"Well, now. The privacy act forbids me from saying anything..." The vet tapped the address card against his chin. "But if you just guessed somebody who might be good with money..."

"You mean Martin Thorpe? The accountant?" Marjorie almost said *my* accountant, but it hadn't been true for the past three months. Not since Martin announced he was downsizing his business prior to retirement and gave her somebody else's number. The new man was perfectly adequate but an unwelcome change all the same.

"I'll get my receptionist to call him. Do you want to wait with Shadow until Martin comes?"

Remembering her ride home had departed, Marjorie nodded. "That'll be good."

A few minutes later, Walter returned with a pensive expression on his face. "No answer."

"You can keep him in overnight if you need to, can't you?"

"It's not ideal for a kitten this young since there'll be nobody to check on him till morning." Walter leant over to pet Shadow under the chin. "And we're about to close."

"What if I take him? I can pop around to Martin's to see why he's not answering his phone and keep him supervised overnight if I need to."

"That'd be great." Walter gave a satisfied nod. "And we'll keep trying his number until we close up for the night."

"Did you hear that, boy?" Marjorie lifted the kitten into the air, prompting some startled paddling from big paws. "You're coming with me."

As Marjorie walked into the waiting room, she fumbled her phone out of her pocket. Although she'd juggled kittens for years, it hadn't made her dextrous. She sat in a chair near the door and thumbed in Braden's number.

Straight to voicemail. Great.

With a sigh, Marjorie eyed the distance from the vet's office to the community centre near the middle of the village. If she kept a firm handle on Shadow, the walk wouldn't take her more than a few minutes.

And if Braden wasn't there?

Well, with a centre full of volunteers, Marjorie was certain someone else would be happy to lend a hand. If worse came to worst, an hour's uphill climb to the café would probably do her legs and heart some good.

"Let's get outside and cadge a lift, what do you say?" she whispered to Shadow who seemed remarkably docile considering the day he'd had so far.

Allie saw her approaching the community centre and strode outside, shaking her head. "Braden's gone if that's who you're after. He said there was an urgent zombie horde he needed to dispatch."

Marjorie laughed as the older woman

pulled her mouth down at the corners. "It sounds like important work."

"Sounds like something he should have outgrown by now."

"I don't suppose anyone else could give me a lift up the hill?"

"I can take you."

She turned, surprised to see Jon hovering, wiping his hands on a dirty rag. If he wanted to get them clean, he should have chosen more wisely. To her eyes, the young man had just wiped more grease onto his skin than had been wiped off.

"That'd be lovely," she said, then hesitated, glancing towards Allie. "Are you allowed to drive the van?"

"If his licence is valid, and he's providing a useful service, he can."

Jon had already nodded and muttered, "Yes," by the time Allie finished.

"Swing by Felix and Dotty's place on the way back," she instructed as he jumped into the driver's seat. "Check to see if any further presents have been dropped off."

The young man gave a wave as he accelerated out of the car park. "I didn't get nothing for Christmas when I was young. Don't see why everybody should be expected to reach into their pockets now."

"They do it because it makes them feel good, and it's fun to pick out presents for children," Marjorie answered, uncertain if he'd even been addressing the complaint to her. "And I'm sorry if you missed out as a child, but it doesn't mean these youngsters should."

"Yeah, alright. I don't need a lecture." Jon shook his head, the greasy brown locks flying. "S'bad enough I have to work from sunup to sundown."

"Doesn't it make you feel great?" she asked, genuinely interested. "The work you do at the community centre is important. It impacts on everyone in town."

"Yeah, I guess," was the sullen reply, though Jon's chest puffed out a little with pride.

"I'm at the top of this road," Marjorie instructed. "Just past the building site."

"I know where you live." The words made her feel a little uneasy but soon Jon followed up with a gruff, "Everyone in this town knows everything about everybody."

"They sure do. It can be a blessing as often as it's a curse."

He dropped her outside, giving a short wave as he turned the van around and headed for Felix's house. Marjorie cuddled Shadow to her chest as she pulled out her keys and headed inside.

The welcome she received was excited enough to tell her she'd missed normal feeding time. Monkey Business loudly explained exactly how late along with an extensive rundown on how it had affected every single one of them.

At least, Marjorie presumed that's what his constant yowling signified since it went on until she finished filling up their bowls and his mouth became otherwise engaged.

"Now, fill up your tummy, then we'll head home and see if your owner's about." Marjorie rubbed the back of her neck and yawned as she waited for Shadow to finish eating. If Martin was home, he was about to get a piece of her mind.

Bad enough to let a full-grown cat loose in the neighbourhood. Letting a kitten out of his eyesight for so long was far worse.

Of course, she should get his side of the story first. With a rueful smile, Marjorie recalled Houdini, a kitten she'd fostered for a time. He'd loved nothing more than slipping out while she wasn't looking, as though her home was a full-time escape room challenge.

"But if he doesn't have a good excuse, he'd better settle in for a long lecture."

Shadow soon polished off the contents of his bowl, leaving her wondering how long it'd been since he'd last eaten. As soon as his hunger was satisfied, the kitten clung close to her heels, pressing against her ankles and nudging the back of her legs when she walked.

"You'll trip me if you're not careful," Marjorie exclaimed, lifting Shadow up and cuddling him since it seemed safer. Monkey protested the arrangement immediately, turning his back and sticking his nose in the air as though in a huff.

"Home time. When the Persian says you've outstayed your welcome, I have to listen." Marjorie popped the Lykoi into a carrier and set off on foot for the short walk to Martin's house.

"Knock, knock," she called out, accompanying the words with the action. "Anybody home?"

After the second try, she walked around the side of the house, pushing past a stubborn branch to reach the side gate. With another call going unanswered, Marjorie walked into the back of the property and came to a halt.

Martin Thorpe's body lay on the concrete, a ladder tipped on its side nearby.

CHAPTER THREE

Marjorie put the pet carrier down, facing away from Martin, and dialled emergency. She didn't need to check the body for signs of life. The one snapshot her eyes took of the scene was enough to convince her he was dead.

"Ambulance," she said to the dispatcher, then immediately second-guessed herself. "Or the police. A man's died."

With the assurance both were on their way, the pleasant-voiced responder asked a series of questions, few of which Marjorie could answer. While concentrating on what the address was and whether any of the doors and windows were unlocked, the time passed and soon a police vehicle pulled into the driveway.

"Getting into trouble again?" Sergeant Matthewson asked in a resigned tone. "Could you show me what you've found?"

"He's around there," Marjorie said, pointing. After having moved through the gate to the front of the house, she had no intention of returning to the horrible scene. One glimpse was enough to ruin her Christmas spirit.

"Don't go anywhere," the sergeant said before disappearing behind the house. Soon Marjorie heard the crackle of his radio, but she couldn't make out any words. Within a minute, another police car arrived, and two uniformed officers walked around the back. Not long after that, a van pulled up and Dr Every—the town pathologist—joined the growing throng.

"Martin in trouble, is he?" a man called out from the footpath. He appeared to be in his fifties, white-haired, dressed as though ready for the golf course, and with his arms folded and a stern expression on his face.

"I probably shouldn't talk about it." Marjorie shifted her weight from one foot to the other, then bent over to check on Shadow who stared out at her with calm resignation. "Are you a friend?"

"Used to be." The man sniffed. "Now Martin and I are just neighbours since he's too good to deal with my business."

"I wouldn't feel bad," Marjorie said, although it appeared the man was already in deep on that score. "Martin severed my business arrangement as well."

"Really?" For the first time, the man looked her full in the face. "I'm Nigel Blythe," he said, sticking out his hand. "You own the kitten café down the road, don't you?"

"That's me. Marjorie Hardaway." She shuffled a step closer to him, preferring the company of a virtual stranger to waiting alone. "I'm afraid Martin's had an accident."

Nigel scanned the property and the police

car before returning his eyes to her face. "Fatal?"

She nodded, unable to trust her voice.

"You found him?"

She nodded again.

"Sorry about that. It must've been a horrid shock." He rubbed at the side of his face where his eyebrow was twitching. "And my apologies if I sounded harsh before. I liked Martin until a few months ago. Since then, it seems like we do nothing but argue."

"About him not handling your accounts any longer?"

Nigel snorted, then put a hand up to cover his nose and mouth, perhaps realising the sound was inappropriate in the circumstances. "No, that wasn't it. I couldn't care less about the numbers, it was just the way he told me, you know? And then his spouting went wonky and sent a constant stream of water into my back yard. Every time I tried to talk to him in a rational tone, it ended up a shouting match."

"Seems everyone in town is on edge, lately."

"You can say that again." Nigel put his hands on his hips and surveyed the street. Another neighbour was out, collecting his mail from the letterbox, and they exchanged a nod before the man walked back indoors. "His ex will be happy at the news."

Marjorie's eyes widened. She didn't hold any candles for her ex-husband either, but she wouldn't be happy to find out he'd died. "Was their relationship that bad?"

"Only with the division of property. Their settlement's been held up in court, time and time again because she reckons Martin's hiding money. She even got one of those forensic accountants in to look over everything."

"I suppose it takes an accountant to know an accountant."

"Yeah." Nigel ran a hand over his face, shaking his head as though to wake himself. "I shouldn't be telling you any of this, should I?

My mother would turn over in her grave to think I'd grown into a gossip."

"Not to worry." Marjorie put a hand on his arm for a second. "It's just the shock talking and I'm not about to tell anyone."

"Good. Thank you." He glanced back at his own driveway. "I should get back since I left my tea cooking on the stove. Did you want to come over to mine if you're waiting for the police?"

"I'm fine here." Marjorie jerked her head in the café's direction. "And I can always head down the road if this takes too long."

He waved goodbye and shuffled back inside, stopping at the doorway for one last glance at the scene. When he'd gone, Marjorie shivered and lifted the cat carrier up to talk to Shadow at face level. "When this is over, you can sit with me in front of the television until it's bedtime."

Sergeant Matthewson emerged from the house not long after. "Sorry about the wait. I'll just grab a few details, then you can be on your way. What are you doing at Mr Thorpe's residence?"

"Returning his pet." Marjorie held Shadow out as evidence. "I found this little one near the café earlier and the vet said he belonged to Martin. I mean, Mr Thorpe." She paused for a second, biting her bottom lip. "When I found the kitten, he was covered in blood."

The sergeant bent over and stared in through the bars of the carrier. Shadow gave him one glance before closing his eyes and falling back to sleep. "Are you able to keep the cat until we establish if a friend or relative wants to take ownership?"

Marjorie nodded. "It's what I was planning to do if Martin wasn't home." She blanched as the scene popped into her head and rubbed her forehead until it disappeared again. "Did he fall?"

"Looks that way, although we won't know anything for sure until the pathologist is through with his investigation. Dr Every doesn't like to give anything away." He cleared his throat and glanced at the open notebook in his hand. "What time did you get here?"

"Six thirty or thereabouts. I usually feed the kittens at five but got caught up with this new arrival so was late. Once that was done, I walked straight here."

"Can you describe what you did once you got here?"

"Knocked on the front door twice and called out. When Martin didn't answer I went around the side and..." She trailed off.

"The gate wasn't locked?"

"No. I just pushed it open."

Sergeant Matthewson's brows drew together, and he frowned at his pad. "It's okay if you did something more to get around the back. Nobody's interested in prosecuting you for breaking and entering. We just want to get all the details straight."

Marjorie had no idea what he was talking about. "I didn't break in." She pointed to the side path as though it would help with the sergeant's understanding. "The gate wasn't locked. I pushed a few branches out of the way and walked around the side, into the back garden."

"Okay." Matthewson snapped his notebook shut and tucked it away. "You haven't seen anyone else about, have you?"

"A neighbour was out here a few minutes ago. Nigel."

The sergeant jerked his head left, then right, and Marjorie nodded at the second gesture. "Right, then. We'll let you get back with what you were doing." He twiddled his fingers at Shadow who still appeared to be sleeping. "And we'll see if we can find someone who wants the cat."

Marjorie walked home in a daze, thrusting unwelcome thoughts out of her head all the way. The moment she walked into her lounge she turned the television on, grateful for the stranger's faces and voices that drowned out the unwelcome visions in her head.

She let Shadow out of the carrier and he promptly glued himself to her heels again, providing the reason for his name. Although she didn't feel much like eating, Marjorie prepared a pot of tea, gulping down a few cups with generous helpings of milk and sugar until she felt more like herself.

Monkey Business strolled into the room and jumped onto the sofa. Judging from the expression on the chocolate Persian's face, he was appalled to find a kitten already seated in Marjorie's lap.

"Don't worry," she said, tickling Monkey behind his ears, just the way he liked. "It's just for this evening. This fellow's had a big shock and I don't think he wants to be alone."

The Persian gave a huff of annoyance but settled beside her, giving Shadow an occasional foul glance. When she regretfully turned off the television, feeling the earlier images crowd back into her head, Marjorie was amused to see Monkey give the Lykoi a bop on the nose when he tried to follow too closely.

"Yes. You are the number one cat around here," she assured him, picking him up for a cuddle and burying her nose into his long fur.

"There's no doubt about that. But cut our new guest a bit of slack, eh?"

Monkey Business rolled his eyes but allowed Shadow to press against her while Marjorie brushed her teeth. She popped the two of them into the kitten pen for sleeping and gave a smile when Monkey pulled the Lykoi close and encircled him while they dozed.

CHAPTER FOUR

"It says here, the breed is a naturally occurring mutation but has only become established in the last few years," Esme read aloud from her phone screen. "There's a breeder in Australia but nothing in New Zealand so far."

"Did you hear that, Shadow?" Marjorie turned and nearly tripped over the closely following kitten. "You might be the first of your breed in the country!"

"Oh, don't say it like that," Esme complained. "It makes him sound so lonely."

Marjorie chuckled. "I said breed, not

species. If he was the only cat in the entire country, then you could get teary over it."

"Martin must've been keen on them to go to so much trouble." Esme squinted at the screen then jumped as the phone broadcast a loud advertisement. "From what I can see, the kittens don't come cheap and there'd be an airfare and clearance from MAF on top of that."

Marjorie couldn't imagine the Ministry for Agriculture and Fisheries would be too concerned over a new breed of cat, but her friend was right about the trouble. Even if it was a rubber stamp approval, it still had to be applied for. There'd also be quarantine and health regulations.

"I don't understand why people can't just pop down to their local animal shelter," she muttered.

"Or their local kitten café," Esme said with a laugh. "People are so weird." She eyed the kitten and picked Shadow off the floor when Marjorie next walked by the table. After giving him a thorough examination, she shook her head. "I don't understand the attraction myself. He's moulting down to bare skin."

"But look at that face!" Marjorie chucked the kitten under the chin and wrinkled her nose as Shadow closed his grey eyes in ecstasy.

"And now his tail's wagging." Esme picked her phone up again. "No wonder they call him a werewolf cat. This one seems to think he's a dog."

"In that case, he'd be the perfect pet for a couple with one dog and one cat person. Think of the arguments he'd spare them."

It was the end of her part of the conversation for a while as a couple near the window drew her attention to a pair of black kittens. They'd arrived in the café the month before and Marjorie had nicknamed them Toil and Trouble.

They loved nothing more than pushing items off the edge of mantels or tables. In the couple's short visit, they'd knocked a napkin, a fork, and a spoon off the place settings, the latter ending up in the woman's purse.

"It's how we know the earth isn't flat," Marjorie said as she cleared up the items and replaced the cutlery. "If it were, kittens would've pushed everything off it by now."

The well-worn joke landed weakly. The spoon had been used to add jam onto the tops of the couple's scones and made everything inside the purse sticky.

"Either behave for the rest of the morning," Marjorie scolded as she herded the kittens to the other side of the café, "or you'll be locked in kitten jail upstairs."

The threat sailed over the pair's heads as they immediately conspired to topple a feather toy off the nearest windowsill. As it landed softly on the carpet below, the two stared in adoration at the sight.

"I hope they go to the same home," Esme remarked as Marjorie came back to her table. "They make quite the pair."

"They do." Marjorie sat and wagged her finger at the two kittens. "It's always nice to see kittens making friends. They turned up two days apart from two different rescues, yet they might as well be siblings."

"I wonder if the breeder in Australia knows about a potential home for your new arrival," Esme said, continuing to scroll through the feed. "If there've been other local enquiries, it might be a simple placement. Especially if it saves someone the expensive price tag."

"I need to wait until the police notify Martin's next of kin." Marjorie felt a paw on the top of her foot and peered over to see Monkey Business with a grim expression on his face. She pulled him into her lap and made a fuss of him. "But the sooner I can rehouse Shadow, the better. It's the first time this one's got possessive."

"How's the Christmas party coming along?" Esme asked, turning her phone face-down on the table. "I heard they're expecting a decent turn-out this year."

"I've worked out a baking list and since I'll be shut the day before, there shouldn't be any problems. It'll just be like my normal morning."

"Let me know if you need a hand with anything." When Marjorie gave her an inquiring glance, Esme shrugged. "I feel bad I can't contribute anything to the party. When I suggested giving out vouchers for a massage, Allie's hair stood on end."

The image made Marjorie giggle until the bell over the door rang, heralding a new arrival. When she rejoined her friend, Esme was watching a video of kittens. "It's research," she protested when Marjorie rolled her eyes. "Look, they're Lykois. They could be Shadow's brothers and sisters, or cousins."

However, the next time Marjorie broke free of her customers, Esme's face was grimmer. "The online news finally has an article about Martin," she said, turning the screen around. "It says he was found by a neighbour."

"I suppose I'm close enough to count as that." Marjorie sat and skimmed the short article, then pushed the phone back towards her friend. "It doesn't look like there's anything new to add."

"They're probably waiting for the reports to come back," Esme said. "There'll be the autopsy report and maybe a toxicology report if they think he might've been under the influence."

When Marjorie raised her eyebrows, Esme shrugged. "What? I watch true crime programs on TV. It's just standard procedure."

"Well, please keep it to yourself. Seeing the real thing has already spun me for a loop."

"You poor thing." Esme leapt to her feet and enveloped Marjorie in a hug. "I'm not trying to be insensitive. If your squeamish stomach needs my big mouth to stay quiet, I'll keep it zipped."

Marjorie disentangled herself with a smile. "You can talk all you like as long as you stick to pleasant subjects. Kittens and string, for example." She jerked her head towards the corner where Toil and Trouble had discovered the delights of yarn.

"Should I get them out of the tangle before they hurt themselves?"

"Maybe let them play a bit longer. It might teach them a valuable lesson."

Esme put Shadow onto the floor and gave his behind a push. "Make friends while you have a captive audience."

The kitten took a few hesitant steps, then turned around and ran for Marjorie's feet instead.

"Honestly! One of these days I'll trip over you and then I'll be dead and how will you like that? Hm?"

It wasn't until she got behind the counter, Marjorie realised Shadow might already have experience in that department. The kitten had attached to her firmly, and she was a virtual stranger. What must it have been like for Martin?

"Don't even think it," Esme said, snapping her fingers. "If I'm not allowed to say things that'll activate your squeamish gene, you're not allowed to think thoughts that do it, either."

The café had almost emptied for the day when Barney Baxter walked inside, looking uncomfortable. "Glad to see you got home okay," he said with forced cheer, taking a stool near the counter. "I just wondered what happened with the kitten."

Marjorie picked up Shadow and plonked him in front of the builder. "He's been fine, and I'd love if you could keep him entertained for a minute."

"You're with the building crew?" Esme asked, seating herself next to him without waiting for an invitation. "I thought you'd be finishing up today."

"Nah." Barney shook his head, then laughed as Shadow copied the movements. "Looks like I've got Ugly Kitten as a mimic."

"Don't call him that," Marjorie said, flicking a teatowel his way. "Just because he doesn't have as much fur as the other kittens, doesn't make him ugly."

Barney held his hands up in surrender. "Whatever you say." As Marjorie clicked her tongue, he turned his attention back to Esme.

"The pour is taking longer than we expected but we'll be out of your hair next week."

"That's good. I guess you've all got families back home expecting you for Christmas?"

The man went still, then winked at Marjorie. "Seems like your friend is angling for information as to my marital status. Do you want to tell her I'm happily married with one kid in primary school and another on the way?"

"I'm sure you're capable of telling her that yourself and I can assure you, no one's 'angling' for your marital status. We're both taken in that regard already."

"Ah-huh." While Esme looked appalled, Barney had a good laugh at her expense. "Don't worry, I was just joking."

Marjorie planted her hands on her hips. "I'm more worried that your schedule of works seems to have been a joke. How much is the delay going to add to my bill?"

Actually, Shaun Hayes was the one financing the building works while Marjorie would share in the eatery he put into the new development, but the builder didn't need to know that.

Not that hiding it made any difference.

"Don't look at me for costs. All that business goes through the lead contractor, so I wouldn't have a clue. I'm just hoping we don't have another time overrun. If I miss Christmas, my wife won't be keen on me coming home at all."

Esme's face said she had the perfect retort for that statement, but Marjorie was pleased she held her tongue.

"What were you after?" Marjorie asked since Barney hadn't ordered anything or even picked up a menu.

"Just checking in on the kitten and you." He slapped his palms on the counter, playing a short riff. "But if you needed me to take care of any leftovers for free"—he tipped a wink at Marjorie—"then I wouldn't say no."

"The leftovers are going to the city mission." Marjorie tipped her head to one side as she studied Barney's reaction. "If that changes your request."

The builder's face scrunched up as he weighed the pros and cons. "They'd lose out if I paid for a muffin now, though, wouldn't they?" he finally said. "So whether I actually pay makes no difference."

"It does to me." Marjorie pointed at the Lykoi sniffing the counter near Barney's elbow. "His food doesn't come free."

Barney pulled his wallet out of his jeans pocket with an awkwardness that suggested he didn't perform the gesture often. "Go on, then. Bad enough the kitten's ugly, I don't want it to starve as well."

He handed across a few gold coins and pointed to the last double chocolate muffin in the display case. Marjorie didn't bother to tell him the cat he was so intent on insulting was worth about two thousand times the cost of his snack. "Pleasure doing business with you, Barney."

She shooed him out of the café just in time to jump as a cup shattered on the floor. When Marjorie turned around, she saw two black kittens feigning sleep, curled around each other in a yin-yang symbol on the floor.

"You'd better adopt out that pair, sharpish," Esme said with a grin, waving goodbye from the doorway. "Otherwise, you'll have to put your prices up and no one in town will ever forgive you for doing that!"

CHAPTER FIVE

"We forgot to ask about allergies, didn't we?" Marjorie said to Monkey Business an hour later as she sat to work out the Christmas baking schedule. Although she'd told Esme she had the situation in hand, the roster wasn't confirmed down to the last minute, the way she preferred. And now she'd discovered what could be a nasty bungle.

The café was easy to operate when it came to allergies. If a customer was allergic to any regular ingredients, they were out of luck.

As a happy coincidence, the clients who

were keen on kittens with their coffee were also largely unafflicted by food allergies. Over the five years she'd been in business, Marjorie could count the number of abstentions for that reason on the fingers of one hand.

But a community event was a different story. The youngsters attending had the right to eat without fear the food would hurt them. It was one thing to have a mouthful spat out because of taste preferences, quite another if it was harmful. Even if not to the point of life-threatening anaphylaxis.

"I must write these ideas down when I have them," she told the chocolate Persian who appeared perturbed by the conversation. "Even if it's the middle of the night."

Although Shadow tried to cling to her, prompting Monkey Business to do the same, Marjorie thought this task was one she could better handle alone. "Why don't you think about what you want for Christmas and I'll be back before you know it?"

The kittens wouldn't know the significance of the date, but Marjorie had stocked up with a few treats throughout the year as money allowed. They were stashed in the top cupboard beside her bed, far away from prying kitty eyes.

It was hard to buy gifts when she had no idea from one day to the next who would be in her care by the time the day arrived. Luckily, her wealth of experience lent her some knowledge of universally approved feline staples.

Santa would deliver ten stockings on Christmas morning, even if she had to stay up all night to do it.

"There's one child who can't abide peanuts," Allie said in response to Marjorie's question a few minutes later. "But I can't think if that's because she's allergic or if she just doesn't like the taste."

"Won't there be records somewhere?"

"I'm sure Oranga Tamariki has records on all that stuff." Allie gave a short laugh. "Let me give you a number to call. I'd offer but conversations with government departments just aren't my thing."

"They're not mine either but better safe than sorry."

As she dialled the number, Marjorie moved closer to the entrance. Just as she received an out-of-office reply, Jon strode through on a mission to somewhere, and nearly bowled her over.

"Sorry," she said, disconnecting the call while he mumbled something under his breath. "You're working late."

"What are you doing here?" Allie called out. "I told you to head on home after setting up the tree."

"Just checking there wasn't anything else that needs fixing." The young man sniffed and wiped his nose on the back of his hand. "You said the decorations would take a long time. Should I get started on them?"

"Tomorrow," Allie said, steering Jon back outside. "And we'll need another coat of paint on the wall before you start tree decorating."

"He's been hanging around outside again," Jon said. "The man who graffitied the wall. I don't see why the police didn't make him paint it over."

"Because he's about four months away from a conviction and sentencing," Allie said, suppressing a smile. "As you well know, given your experience of the court system." She turned to head inside, rolling her eyes at Marjorie, then spun around with her finger-wagging. "And don't you talk to him, neither. You give him any encouragement and he'll just be at it again."

Jon shoved his hands deep into the pockets of his jeans. "I'm not about to make work for myself. There's enough to go around as it is." He sloped off, casting a scowl at a middle-aged man who stood on the edge of the car park.

"He doesn't seem like any trouble," Marjorie observed.

"Who? Jon?"

"No." Marjorie pointed to the sad figure standing outside. "The graffiti artist."

"I'm sure he's all smiles and sunshine until something doesn't go his way." Allie slammed the door shut. "I've got a good mind to call the police to move him on."

Marjorie sidled up to the nearest window and peeked outside. "Looks like he's got the message." The man was striding away, shoulders slumped in dejection.

"It's ridiculous. We're hosting a party not holding his son ransom." Allie ran a hand through her short hair, puffing air out of her mouth. "Perhaps I should call the police, anyway. Given the damage he already did to the centre, I would've thought they'd issue an order to keep him far away."

"Maybe they did." Marjorie dialled the non-urgent station number. "Regina? I'm down at the community centre and a man who caused damage earlier is hanging around outside. We're checking to see if there's something we can do."

PC Regina Ashcroft's response had Marjorie holding the phone away from her ear to protect it from damage. She winked at Allie. "I take it he's not meant to come near here, then?"

After a short discussion, Marjorie hung up the phone. "The police trespassed him from the centre when they released him, so he's not meant to come within one hundred metres of the place. Regina said if you see him again, don't hesitate to call."

"Well, that's good to know." Allie moved nearer the window. "It doesn't explain why Jon's still hanging about." She tapped on the glass, but the young man didn't appear to hear her. "First, he doesn't want to come here at all, now I can't get him to leave."

"What's his home life like? Everyone seems to be stressed about Christmas this year, have you noticed? Perhaps he's avoiding going home." Marjorie put her hand on the doorknob. "I'll engage him in conversation on my way out. That should send him scurrying."

But Jon headed away before she could catch up to him. While fumbling to unlock her car door, a woman cleared her throat behind her and Marjorie turned, squinting. "Can I help you?"

The lady was around Marjorie's age but

could have been older considering the aura of wealth that surrounded her. Money usually lent people confidence as well, but that gift appeared to have bypassed her altogether.

She wrung her hands together, a diamond engagement ring that could have paid for Marjorie's house and café sparkling in the early evening light. "I have a load of Christmas gifts in my car for the party," she said in a high, thin voice. "Do you know where I should take them?"

"It's just through that door there," Marjorie said pointing. When the woman followed her finger but didn't make a move, she offered, "Can I give you a hand taking them inside?"

"That'd be lovely. I'm Lillian Skinner." The woman held out her hand to shake.

"Did you miss the collection?" Marjorie fell into step beside her. "Felix and Dotty went around the neighbourhood in the van, picking things up."

"I was at the hairdressers and my son didn't let them inside." Lillian shook her head, pressing her lips in a thin line. "I'm not sure if it was to spite me or if he was abiding by our warnings about strangers."

"How old's your son?"

"Fourteen."

Marjorie laughed. "Unless he's still waiting for his growth spurt, I doubt he had anything to fear from those two."

"That's what I thought, too, but I'm not allowed to say." Lillian shot a quiet smile towards Marjorie, who reciprocated.

"The presents aren't wrapped, are they?" she asked, thinking back to the day before.

"Not yet." Lillian gave a small shake of her head as she opened the back of her four-wheel drive, revealing a mountain of neatly stacked boxes. "Though, if it was up to my husband, every single gift would have a tag specifying how much it cost and that it was generously donated by him."

"A true philanthropist, is he?"

Lillian burst into laughter, then put a hand to her mouth and glanced around with wary eyes. "Claude always ensures credit when credit's due. Even with charity."

"The kids won't care," Marjorie said when the woman seemed upset. "And if you think he'll be more likely to donate again next year if he receives effusive praise for his generosity, then I'm happy to write him a letter on behalf of the centre."

"Really?" Lillian briefly closed her eyes. "That would be great."

They manhandled the large stack of gifts inside the community hall, with Marjorie making a mental note to tell Braden he could put his wrapping skills to use again in the morning.

"Are you attending the party?" she asked Lillian on their way out and the woman shrugged. "If you are coming, let me know what your favourite dessert is, and I'll bake it special."

Based on the hand that flew to Lillian's waist and the pained expression on her face, Marjorie guessed dessert wasn't something she indulged in.

"What a pity," she told Monkey Business

when she arrived home. "If I had a rich husband, I'd eat until I was twice the size I am, then pay a plastic surgeon to suction all my fat back out!"

Braden wasn't answering his phone so Marjorie settled for a text message, figuring his idea of early in the morning wouldn't be before ten. If Esme had as few clients booked tomorrow as she did the rest of the week, hopefully, she wouldn't mind watching the café while Marjorie snuck off to wrap presents with her boyfriend.

"That's my idea of a neat date," she said to Shadow, who still clung dangerously close to her heels. "My teenage self would be sad beyond words."

Monkey Business trotted over and pushed Shadow's head into the floor, taking his place as he skittered away.

"Monkey! Be nice!"

The Persian jumped back with a shocked expression, but Marjorie wasn't falling for his act. "Shadow might be as annoying as a little sibling to you, but you have to treat him with care. He's been through a lot lately and doesn't need you bullying him."

Monkey turned and walked away, nose in the air. As soon as he was out of reach, Shadow hurried back to take up residence at Marjorie's feet. "The sooner we find a new home for you, the better."

THE NEXT MORNING was drizzling and Marjorie was kept busy with builders sheltering until they could get to work on the site next door. She poured mug after mug of strong tea served with full-fat milk and sold out of scones before her usual customers could get a look in.

With all the rushing, Marjorie was happy that Barney took temporary ownership of 'the ugly cat,' so she didn't have him tangling around her feet. Unfortunately, a clingy Monkey Business soon took up residence, mimicking Shadow though he was usually happy to stay in the corner, playing.

"You know I'll always love you," she said, popping him in the playpen although she knew he'd escape in ten seconds' flat. "You don't have to be jealous."

Luckily the head builder took an interest in the chocolate Persian and distracted the kitten long enough for her to get through the queue of orders.

When the rain lifted and she could take a breather, Marjorie saw a reply to her message of the day before on her phone. She smiled as she picked it up, nearly tossing it when the phone unexpectedly rang in her hand. "Hello?"

"It's Braden. I'm at the community centre and everyone's shell-shocked."

"Why? What happened?"

He gulped and blurted out the terrible news. "The Christmas gifts have been stolen."

CHAPTER SIX

Marjorie left the café in Esme's capable hands and rushed to the community centre. In the five months they'd been dating, she'd never heard Braden sound so emotional. When she stormed through the door, he stood with his back against the wall, his face drained of colour.

"Is anybody hurt?" she cried, spinning to include Allie, Felix, Dotty, and Jon in her question. "How did they get in?"

"We think they jimmied a window," Allie said in a flat voice. Her shoulders slumped and her energy seemed to have slipped down to the floor. "There's some splintering on a sill out the back but we're waiting for the police to arrive and confirm."

"They haven't attended yet?" Marjorie was shocked.

"With the murder—"

Marjorie interrupted, "What murder?"

Allie glanced at Felix who turned bright red. "It's not common knowledge," he mumbled under his breath.

"You're talking about Martin?"

He nodded and wrapped an arm around Dotty's waist. "I dropped by the station yesterday with this one"—he jerked his chin at Jon—"to sign in and heard the sergeant talking about the pathology report."

"I've told you a hundred times not to eavesdrop." Dotty folded her arms and frowned but didn't remove the arm around her.

"They shouldn't have been talking so loud about private things," Felix protested, rubbing behind his ear. "Anyway, the injuries he sustained aren't consistent with a fall. That's all I know."

"I can't believe someone would murder that nice young man," Dotty said with a sniff. "This town used to be a safe place to retire or bring up young kids. Now the papers are stuffed full of crime instead of tips on growing the best tomatoes."

"Most of the stories are from Christchurch," Felix said giving her a bump with his hip. "You know that."

"So we've got a cesspool of crime brewing a ninety-minute drive away. You're hardly making things better. Besides, our Chrissy presents weren't in Christchurch. They were in the next room."

Marjorie's mind buzzed with the news about Martin Thorpe. The man had been pleasant and helpful in his role as her accountant. Despite his standoffish nature, she'd always presumed they'd eventually become firm friends. Even after he dropped her business.

Too late now.

"You don't suppose the murderer was at his house when I found the body?" she asked in horror as the thought crowded into her head. "While I was standing outside waiting for the police, the killer could have escaped."

Braden touched the back of her hand and shook his head. "From what you've said, Martin's body must've been lying there for a while. How long would it take his kitten to walk all the way from his house to the building site?"

"I suppose." Marjorie pressed a palm to her forehead, which felt hot. "And I should concentrate on the presents. That's a crime we might be able to solve."

"We'll have no option if the police don't get a move on," Felix snapped. "We've been waiting for close on an hour."

Marjorie turned to Allie. "Were they missing when you arrived at work?"

"Probably." Two spots of colour burned high on her cheeks. "But Jon and I were outside, getting the final coat of paint over the graffiti. It took us a couple of hours to finish, then we came inside for a spot of tree decorating and found everything gone."

"Do you mind if I look?"

The group shook their heads and Marjorie walked across the room, resisting the urge to tiptoe. From the doorway, she could see the enormous pile of presents that she and Lilliana had added to the previous evening were gone. The tree, the spare wrapping paper and ribbons, and the bicycles donated for two lucky youngsters had been left behind.

"What about the consoles?" she asked, walking back to join Braden. "Are they still in the games room?"

He nodded tiredly. "They're still there and so is all the food stored in the kitchen freezers."

Marjorie would never even have thought to check, but she understood the concern. With dozens of guests coming, the investment in ham, turkey, and trimmings was substantial.

"They're pretty dumb thieves to leave behind those two bikes," she said, tilting her head back so the approaching tears would be forced to retreat. "And the computer equipment."

"I think they might've been interrupted," Felix said. "The wrapped presents were an easy grab because they were all stacked up together. The other stuff would have taken another trip."

Braden nodded. "It makes sense. Hopefully, the police can track down who saw them and get it sorted quickly."

"But catching the thieves won't get the Christmas presents back." When the group turned to Marjorie, she continued, "Nobody would steal a pile of toys for no reason. They've probably opened and tossed aside everything they didn't want."

"Like the world's greediest children," Braden added sadly. "Either way, we need to work out what to give the kids now. Apart from a big lunch and a games room."

"Perhaps we can canvass the local

businesses again," Marjorie suggested. "If they donated gifts previously, they might be in the mood to donate again. Especially given what's happened."

"But the biggest donors have already shut up shop," Allie said, her face twisted with misery. "The most generous companies aren't trading right up to Christmas day. They've already closed with no plans to reopen until after New Year's."

"But we've still got Monday and Tuesday to go next week." Marjorie shook her head at the luxury of being able to shut for a fortnight until the festive season had been and gone.

"Most of the business district take two weeks off. Even the ones running a skeleton crew operate out of Christchurch and don't have anyone on the ground, here."

"What about the bars and restaurants?" Marjorie looked to Felix and Dotty who'd done most of the legwork the first time around. "If they didn't contribute originally, they might be willing to help now."

"They've donated food to the event, just like you. Adding gifts on top of it..." Allie trailed off and frowned at the floor.

Marjorie became more downcast as each potential remedy failed but she wasn't quite done yet. "Door to door?"

"We don't have time," Allie shouted, stamping one foot on the floor before pacing over to glare out the window. "Even if we could get the money for gifts, we've still got to go over the list and select the right presents for each child. All that takes hours, you know."

"The list is still there from our first rally," Dotty said, ignoring her friend's outburst. "But without the financing, we're stuck."

Regina pulled up outside in a police car, ending the conversation for the time being. She cheerfully went through the motions of investigating the scene, even roping off the room with a short piece of police tape.

"Who was the last person to leave the centre last night?" she asked when she'd checked the room and the presumed point of entry thoroughly. When Allie raised a hand, Regina took her aside for a flurry of questions. Although Marjorie couldn't hear the conversation, she saw the way Regina's eyes kept returning to Jon.

"You called yesterday about Evan Westcott hanging around outside?" Regina said, finishing up with Allie and striding across to Marjorie. "Did he leave?"

"Is he the one who tagged the building?" When Regina nodded, Marjorie continued, "Yeah, but he walked away while I was talking to you."

"Have you seen him since?"

"I've only just turned up." She glanced over to Allie who shook her head. "Do you think he'd be the type to steal presents?"

"The man isn't in his right mind." Allie walked over to join Marjorie. "His son is due to attend the party with his foster parents. Since Evan thought nothing of spray-painting the side of the building, I guess he might be petty enough to steal the presents, so everybody has as bad a day as he does."

Marjorie jumped as though hit with a physical blow. She wanted to deny the allegation, even though she didn't know the man. It was a terrible thought that someone could set out to ruin the day for a group of underprivileged kids.

On the other hand, the gifts cost a lot of money and took time to organise, but no one would make much money selling them, especially on the black market. If cash was ruled out as a motive, then it didn't leave much else.

"People are so awful." Allie burst into tears. "How could someone do this just before Christmas? Why ruin the party for everyone?" She wiped her face with the back of her hand, heat rising in her cheeks. "I've spent half my life volunteering for this community and every year it gets harder. This is the final straw!"

She stormed out the door, kicking it shut behind her. The behaviour was so out of character Marjorie felt shaken to her core.

Braden tugged at his earlobe. "Should we go after her?"

"Leave her alone," Dotty said in a firm tone. "She's been wound tight as a drum all year, so it'll do her good to let off a bit of steam."

Marjorie thought it would also do the woman good to know how much everyone appreciated and loved her, and leaving her alone to shout and cry in the car park was no way to show that. But Felix and Dotty knew Allie much better. After a moment of hesitation, she deferred to their judgement.

"Felix thought the burglars might've been interrupted halfway through," Marjorie said to Regina, trying to get things back on track. "Would there be CCTV showing the incident?"

"Oh, yeah." The officer pointed across the road, then next door. "We've got two angles on the car park if they were stupid enough to use it. Another one around the back where the window's been tampered with." Regina rubbed her eyes. "Since there won't be much action on a Thursday night, if they used a vehicle and parked nearby, we'll soon find them." She sighed and tapped her pen on her notepad. "I doubt we're dealing with a master criminal, but I don't know that we'll recover anything. At least, not in a fit state for the children."

Jon scowled and folded his arms over his chest, rocking back and forward against the wall. After a moment, he pushed away and strode outside, heading in a different direction than Allie.

"I hope that lad doesn't think his community service is done just because his boss took a minute to regain her composure," Felix said in a slow drawl. "Because if he does, he's got another think coming."

"Unless anyone has more information," Regina said, "then I'll be on my way. I'll have a word with Mr Roscoe on my way out and remind him he's not here by choice."

However, it was too late. With a screech of tyres, Jon drove the community centre van out of the car park, clipping the curb as he pulled onto the road and headed away.

Regina cleared her throat. "I don't suppose anyone can account for Jon's whereabouts at the time of the break in?"

CHAPTER SEVEN

"It was awful," Marjorie said later to Esme, burying her face in her hands. "I feel so sorry for those poor kids even crying doesn't help."

"Good." Esme undid her apron and tossed it in the hamper. "Because crying won't get anything useful done. What we need to do is rally the community into replacing the presents. We mightn't be able to afford to replace name-brand stuff, but we can still make sure every kid gets a nice toy to play with."

"I wondered about going door to door and asking for donations," Marjorie began but Esme shook her head.

"It's too close to Christmas to ask for charity. People will stretch every dollar to provide the best holiday they can for themselves. What we should do is sell them something they need and use the profits for the replacement gifts."

"And what do people need?"

"A massage to unwind or a quick sugar fix to make them feel better. I'd blocked off my calendar for next week anyway, so I've got time to spare. If we take some of your muffins and biscuits around, we'll soon be in profit, I bet you."

"We can try," Marjorie said, biting her lip in doubt.

Esme laughed and clapped her on the shoulder. "Take a friendly kitten with you to seal the deal. A mobile kitten café should increase conversions no end."

"Only if you take your mobile massage

chair to perform a shoulder massage on the spot. If we're trying to relieve the stress of Christmas, then you need to deliver right away. It'll just increase pressure if folks have one more appointment to remember."

"Good point." Esme hooked up an eyebrow. "Food, massages, and a kitten cuddle. Sounds like the perfect recipe for anyone who needs a dose of relaxation in their life."

"Tomorrow afternoon?"

"Why not today?"

Marjorie wrinkled her nose and grinned. "Because I need to bake supplies and gather up some energy. After the shock of this morning, I'll last about three houses before I'll be the one sitting in your massage chair."

"You should bring the terrible twins along," Esme said with a nod towards Toil and Trouble, who were busy shuffling a saltshaker off a nearby table. "They can push the customers towards a sale."

She left on Marjorie's groan.

THE NEXT MORNING, Marjorie decided halfway through her baking run to take Monkey Business along for the jaunt. Shadow was clinging to her for dear life while the chocolate Persian glared daggers at him from the nearby sofa.

"If I bring you, promise you'll behave yourself," she said, giving him a quick cuddle. "Because if you're snippy then we won't make any sales and the foster kids will have to go without."

Monkey looked suitably chagrined—a neat trick but one which Marjorie didn't trust for a second. "I'm serious. At the first sign of mischief, I'm putting you in a cat carrier and you'll be in timeout for the rest of the evening."

Knowing she had a lot of walking to look forward to later, Marjorie rested as much as she could with a café full of harried customers. As one couple stumbled inside, clinging onto a half dozen shopping bags, she had to rush over and hold the door. "Wouldn't you feel more comfortable leaving those in the car?"

"Didn't you hear?" the woman said with a sniff. "There's a Christmas thief about stealing everyone's presents."

"That's why we've left the shopping till the last minute," her husband agreed. "If we had to worry about this haul being left alone while we were at work, it'd stress us into an early grave."

"Well, at least let me store them behind the counter, out of your way," Marjorie said, feeling a pang of regret that such fear existed in her town. "You'll have a full view of them while being able to enjoy your coffee."

The suggestion went down so well, she soon repeated it as more customers arrived with bundles under their arms. An hour before closing, she finally thought to place out a jar for donations in case the same news would prompt generosity as well as fear.

"Ready?" Esme called out as Marjorie hauled the sign indoors. "I've got my best walking shoes on."

Jerry strolled through the door after her, rolling his eyes. "And don't make me tell you the battle I fought to get her to wear them. Somebody seemed to think high-heeled sandals were fitting footwear."

"Did somebody?" Esme poked her partner in the ribs with a chuckle. "I was just thinking I'd get more people taking me up on my offer if I was stylish."

"Are you coming along, Jerry?"

He shook his head. "I've been banned from the venture, even though I offered to be the muscle. Just remember"—he turned to Esme —"if that cumbersome chair grows too heavy, I've got my phone turned on and charged up, ready for your call."

The portable 'massage chair' wasn't actually that large. It affixed onto an existing chair to provide a comfortable padded spot for customers to lay their faces while their masseuse worked behind them.

"It's only balsa wood," Esme said with a tone that suggested she'd already been through this a dozen times before. "And we won't be going far."

"Unless we strike out with all the neighbours," Marjorie said, voicing her main concern.

"That's not the spirit I was hoping for," her friend replied. "Now, are you going to be okay carrying all your baking?"

"I'm taking a trolley." Marjorie pulled it out. Stainless steel practicality festooned with Christmas tinsel. "And once I've sold a few batches, you'll be able to perch your chair on top."

"You see?" Esme pushed Jerry's chest and avoided his face as he leaned in for a kiss. "We'll be fine. You're worrying about nothing."

They struck out at the first few houses, but when they knocked on Gwen Chalmers door, the lady clapped her hands. "You're a godsend," she declared, purchasing three packets of Marjorie's gingerbread men and waving her hand when she tried to find change. "Don't worry about a few coins. I thought my head would explode when Charles called to say he was bringing a few mates over for a barbeque. The man doesn't seem to understand some events take planning!"

At the next house along, a housewife on the verge of tears took advantage of Esme's ten-minute neck and shoulder massage. Marjorie happily exchanged gossip about the building site with the woman's husband while he repaid her with a cup of tea.

"I should remember this for next year," Marjorie said as she sold out of the gingerbread men and started selling her triple chocolate biscuits in earnest. "At this rate, I'll equal the day's takings in an hour."

Esme flexed her fingers out and grinned in delight. "Didn't I tell you? Stressed people confined to their homes are always desperate for sugar and massages."

"You did." Marjorie slowed as they passed

Martin's house. "The poor man. I wonder why there's a car in the driveway?"

"We have the perfect excuse to find out," Esme declared, dragging on Marjorie's hand when she tried to demur. "Don't be an old fogie."

Monkey Business seemed happy to let his owner be pulled against her will and jumped to the front of the trolley for the short, bumpy ride.

"Stop looking so suspicious," Esme hissed as she knocked on the front door. "You might as well hang a sign out saying 'I'm not meant to be here.'"

"There's no one home," Marjorie said with a sigh of relief after a few seconds passed with no reply. "Let's move on."

"Hello?" a woman said, pulling the door open. "Can I help you?"

"Are you Ingrid Thorpe?" Esme asked with no apparent shame while Marjorie tried to make herself as small as possible. "I'm so sorry to hear about Martin."

"I've gone back to my maiden name, Littleman," Ingrid said, shaking the hand Esme thrust at her. "And yes. It's been quite a shock."

"We're selling massages and biscuits," Esme said, pushing inside. "I can give you a lovely neck and shoulder massage. It'll be just the treat if you're carrying any stiffness in your upper body."

"Oh well, I—"

"You must be devastated about your ex. Even when you're having a messy divorce and say you want your partner dead, I don't think anybody really means it."

"What? I never—"

"Not you. I just meant anyone who goes through a breakup. Are you moving back into the house or are you selling?"

Ingrid seemed taken aback by the rapid-fire questioning and Marjorie couldn't blame her. She rarely saw Esme in full gossip-collecting mode and found it distinctly uncomfortable.

"I'm selling," Ingrid managed after a long

pause. "Since Martin and I split up, I've made a new life for myself down in Timaru."

"Oh, that's a lovely place. I heard you got in a forensic accountant to look over the financial details, is that true?"

Marjorie gasped. "Esme!"

"What? I'm just asking."

"It's none of our business."

Ingrid's eyes flicked between them, her face growing more confused by the second. "Who told you that?"

"Martin," Esme said while Marjorie's cheeks flushed with colour. She couldn't stand on the high ground when she'd told her friend what Nigel had told her.

"Yes, it's true." Ingrid frowned at the trolley as Monkey Business grew bored with the conversation and declared his intention to nap with a loud yawn. "I'll take a packet of those biscuits. I haven't had a minute to myself since I drove up this morning and I'm starving."

She walked into the kitchen after this

pronouncement and the two women took it as an invitation to follow. Marjorie passed her the biscuits and considered not charging since Esme seemed determined to extract information as payment. But they were doing this for a good cause, so she tossed the impulse aside.

Ingrid tore open the cellophane and offered the biscuits around while the kettle was boiling. "You want a cup of tea? I'd offer you coffee, but Martin only had instant and it's honestly not worth the trouble."

Having already accepted an offer of tea once on their journey, Marjorie declined. If she had one more, her back teeth would start floating.

"I didn't want to get all nasty during the divorce," Ingrid said after polishing off two biscuits in a row. "But I know for certain that Martin had more assets than he declared to the courts. I asked him over and over to just front up with the true numbers, but he kept insisting he had." She shrugged. "I had no choice but to hire an accountant. After putting twenty years of my time and earnings into our marriage, I wasn't about to be cheated just because my husband is better at hiding his assets than I am."

"Fair enough, too," Marjorie said, remembering the painstaking settlement that she'd received as part of her divorce. Being a failure at marriage was hard enough. Feeling like your ex-partner had got the better of you in the decree would be unbearable.

"How did you know he had more money than he declared?" she asked. "Did the bank account balances suddenly go down?"

"No, but Martin always contributed at least as much as I did to the joint accounts and suddenly he was declaring half that. He also had his own savings account—well, we both did—but it was mysteriously empty when it came time to settle." Ingrid tipped the last of her tea into the sink and rinsed out the cup. "Then I heard he's got enough funding to let go most of his clients. None of it added up."

"Thank goodness Jerry and I keep separate accounts," Esme said. "I'd hate to think of him scurrying around, hiding money if we split."

"Yeah," Ingrid said, nodding. "Try it when you're counting on the funds to afford a house. I thought I'd chosen a modest dwelling but without the additional income, there's no way I could afford to buy."

"I suppose you're set now."

Marjorie's eyes widened at Esme's words while her friend gave her an innocent stare.

"You mean now my ex-husband's dead?" Ingrid angrily munched her way through another biscuit. "I suppose your next line is to imply I killed him!"

Esme gasped and put a hand to her chest. "The thought never crossed my mind." After a second of silence, she added, "But since we're here…"

"No! Much as I wanted to, I didn't kill Martin. In fact, the police say his death was accidental."

"Well, then. That's good to know."

Marjorie shook her head. "No, it's not good to know, and it's none of our business." She shoved Esme between the shoulder-blades, aiming her at the door. "Thanks for your hospitality and for putting up with my very inquisitive friend, but we'll be on our way now."

"If you're going around the neighbourhood, would you mind very much telling the rest of the street I didn't kill Martin?" Ingrid asked, apparently unfazed. "I've only been back in town a few hours and I've already had three drive-bys with people openly staring."

"We will." Marjorie pushed Esme out the door when it seemed she was about to head back into the kitchen. "Honestly, I don't know how you can be so brazen!"

"It's better than talking about someone behind their back," Esme said with a shrug. "And it's not like you weren't wondering the same thing."

"Well, yes. But I'd be too polite to ask."

"Then it's a miracle you ever find out the truth about anything," Esme declared, walking towards Nigel's house. "At least now, we can tell her neighbours she's not a murderer with some confidence."

Marjorie burst into laughter as she followed along behind, still stunned from the visit. When they got to Nigel Blythe's front door she pushed ahead of Esme, not in any hurry for a repeat performance.

CHAPTER EIGHT

"You remember I told you about the spouting," Nigel said as Esme finished working her magic fingers into his back and shoulders. "About how Martin kept refusing to fix it, so water kept pooling on my side of the fence?"

"I remember." Marjorie was sitting on his kitchen counter. She wouldn't usually be so bold as to jump up on a stranger's bench, but Nigel had chosen Saturday morning to stain all his kitchen chairs and had offered it as the only alternative to standing.

Nigel stretched his arms up to the ceiling

and groaned. "That's about a thousand times better, thank you. What's the occasion you're raising money for?" He handed across Esme's fee, then raised an eyebrow when neither of them answered. "Or is this a private venture?"

"No, it's covering the stolen Christmas gifts from the community centre." Marjorie hopped down from the bench and flexed out her legs. Although they hadn't walked far, the exercise on top of her daily work was making itself known. "And what happened with the spouting?"

"Oh, well." Nigel rubbed at his eyebrow, showing reluctance to elaborate though it was he who'd begun the conversation. "Just, I think I might be responsible for Martin's death."

Marjorie went still. "You do?"

"He sent me a text message. Only, I hadn't checked at the time the police were next door because nobody ever texts me. I don't really understand how to check for them."

Esme gave an amused snort. "How do you know he sent one, then?"

"My phone had an exclamation mark in the corner. When I handed it to the woman in the dairy, she showed me the message."

Marjorie waited for a long pause, then prompted, "Which said?"

"I could chillax because he would fix the spouting."

"Oh, no." Esme wrinkled her nose. "You're definitely going down for the crime, then. That's proof of murder right there."

Nigel's face registered alarm before he realised she was joking. "Ha, ha. I don't mean I killed him with my bare hands."

"You think he fell off the ladder while he was fixing the spouting and that makes it your fault?" Marjorie's mouth twisted. "You know it's not, right?"

"Logically, I suppose." Nigel thumped at his chest. "It feels true here, though, and that's where it counts."

"A friend of ours overheard a conversation at the police station," Esme said after a moment. "It doesn't make the situation any more pleasant, but they think it might be murder." She paused, then added, "Actual murder, that is. Not asking someone to maintain their property like they're meant to, murder."

"No!" Nigel's face drained of all colour. "But I thought he fell."

"So did I." Marjorie picked up Monkey Business and cuddled him close to her. "That's what it looked like."

"Much as I hate to think I had anything to do with Martin's death," Nigel said, "I hope your friend overheard wrong. The last thing we need is a killer stalking the community right on Christmas." He leaned over to pet Monkey on the head. "Are you trying to get this one adopted?"

"No, he's helping." As though the Persian knew they were talking about him, he promptly attacked a corner of the cellophane biscuit wrapping, tearing a neat hole.

"Helping, eh? How much for a damaged packet?"

"The same price as for a whole one. It's for charity so we can't afford to give discounts."

Nigel pulled his wallet back out and handed over the cash. "I'd love to help in some way. I don't suppose you need a website, do you?"

"Is that your line of business?" When Nigel nodded, Marjorie pursed her lips in thought. "What about a fundraiser page? For online donations. Is that something you could organise?"

The man clapped his hands together and nodded. "I sure can. Do you have any photos of the orphans looking sad?"

"They're foster children," Marjorie corrected. "And no."

"There are some photographs from last year's event on the community centre website." Esme followed Nigel through to a home office with computer equipment all around. It reminded Marjorie of Braden's house, though Nigel kept things tidier.

Esme typed in an address and pulled up a range of images from the previous year. "Would they work?"

"They'll do nicely." Nigel sat and started to

type furiously on the keyboard. "Why don't you swing by again in an hour? I should have the main page mapped out by then. If you're happy with the appearance, I can get it live tonight. When's the deadline?"

"We'll need the funds in the account by Tuesday morning if we're to have any hope of driving to Christchurch for the presents and getting back in time to wrap them." Marjorie glanced at Esme. "Unless there's something else I haven't thought of?"

"If I put the cut-off at Monday for donations, that should stream them into the account in time. Do you have the community centre bank number?"

"Nope. But I can call Allie to find out and bring it by later."

"Great." Nigel tapped away at the keyboard for a few seconds. "Anything that comes in after the deadline can go towards next year. The event will happen again then, yeah?"

"I suppose." Marjorie thought of Allie's sadness when she'd met up earlier in the week and her outburst that morning, so out of character. "And if not, we can always donate them to another worthy cause. No one's in this to make money."

"Cool, cool. I'll put a note to that effect." Nigel flapped his hands at them. "Get on, now. Let me concentrate on my work."

It only took another dozen houses for Marjorie to sell out and by then, Esme was flagging. "Let's get on home so I can show Jerry I survived unmolested. You can also phone Allie for the bank account details before we get back to Nigel's."

Based on Jerry's reaction when they returned home, he'd been expecting a call to the morgue to identify Esme's body. While Marjorie hid a grin, he lavished his partner with praise and affection until she warded him off with both hands.

A similar reaction awaited Marjorie, but the tribe of kittens were easier to distract with a few judicious shakes of the kibble container. While they fed, she called Allie and got the details for Nigel, only mentioning the website rather than her and Esme's contribution to the fund.

Monkey Business quickly finished his dinner and lounged next to her on the sofa as she stretched out her legs. Although it wasn't a long distance back to Nigel's, she wondered if Esme would mind taking the car. In the few minutes she'd been resting, large knots had formed in the muscles of her calves and they required judicious massaging to avoid turning into cramps.

"I should teach you how to do this," she remarked to Monkey who nuzzled at her hands for a moment before returning to his chief job of dozing. "Or you," she said to Shadow as he trotted from his empty bowl in a direct line to her seat.

Halfway there, the chocolate Persian jumped to full alertness and sprang into his path, back arching and mouth hissing. With Monkey's long hair standing on air, he was a terrifying sight to behold.

"Hey, now. Calm down." Marjorie patted

her ample stomach. "There's more than enough of me to go around."

But neither cat retreated. They circled each other like prizefighters, then Monkey Business struck the first blow, claws extended.

"Stop it!" Marjorie lifted the Persian up, his entire body as stiff as a board. For a moment, staring into his furious eyes, she thought Monkey would attack her as well but after a second he relaxed, nuzzling up to her neck as though nothing had happened.

Marjorie's whole body shook as she put him into the playpen and caught hold of the Lykoi around the midriff. He seemed happy to be held and the wounds along his side weren't deep enough to draw blood. The scratches would probably be noticeable for a few days, but they weren't life threatening.

"You're coming on a quick journey," she said, popping Shadow into the cat carrier. "It's not your fault but I can't have disharmony in the ranks. If Monkey Business doesn't want you to stay here, then you'll need another home."

She knocked on Esme's door to say she'd be delayed for a few minutes, twenty at most, then drove down the hill while anxiety sent pins and needles along her arms.

"Just so you don't think I'm a mean woman, I'll get onto the breeder and scope out another likely owner for you, since it doesn't appear the ex-Mrs Thorpe has any interest in inheriting you. How does that sound?"

Shadow gave a plaintive mew, identical to the sounds he'd been making when Barney first discovered him. The noise travelled in through Marjorie's ears and tugged at her heart.

"If the breeder doesn't have anyone on her waitlist, then I'll put out a big advertisement, showcasing your many attractive features." She cast a sidelong glance at the cat carrier, having to agree with Barney that between the moulting and the scarce hair coverage, it might take someone with a pure soul to see the kitten's attractiveness.

"And if that doesn't work, I'll go out in person and press the flesh until we find you a good home. You've had a rough start in life, no mistake, but that won't be your entire story. There's a happy end waiting for you."

Marjorie pulled to a halt outside a modest house with sturdy brick construction and a lawn that was masquerading as a field thanks to the early summer heat.

"You'll like your new foster parent," she assured Shadow after knocking on the door. "He's a great man and very laid back. You'll hit it off like a house on fire."

When Braden opened the door, his mussed hair and messy clothing told her she'd interrupted a fuelled stretch of gaming. "Surprise," Marjorie said, holding the cat carrier aloft. "You're the lucky recipient of a foster kitten. Merry Christmas."

CHAPTER NINE

"But I know nothing about taking care of a cat," Braden protested while Marjorie settled Shadow into his living room. "What if I kill him from neglect?"

"You won't. It's not nearly so difficult as you seem to think. Food. Water. Litter tray. Comfort. Every time you eat or drink or go to the bathroom just think, has Shadow got the same opportunities? If the answer's yes, you're fine."

"What about fresh air and sunshine?" Braden ran a hand through his hair, looking so adorably concerned that Marjorie couldn't help but laugh. "I spend most of my time indoors."

"So does he. Shadow is a full-time house cat. Set him up on a cushion next to you when you start gaming, and he'll love it. And he sleeps even longer than you do."

"But…"

Marjorie reached out and took his hand, giving it a reassuring squeeze. "No buts. I'll try my best to rehouse him as soon as possible but I can't have him at home. You're the next best thing."

"Esme. Won't she be better at kitten-sitting?"

"No." Marjorie sighed and put her hands on her hips. "Don't you think I'd have her place festooned with kittens already if she was that way inclined?"

"What if I'm a terrible owner?"

"Then you can take comfort in knowing it's only for a short time. You can always reach me at the other end of a phone call if there's a genuine emergency."

"What counts as genuine?"

"Anything where the four things I mentioned won't cut it. If he gets sick or doesn't act like himself."

"How am I meant to know how he should act?"

She stared at him with an eyebrow raised. "If you're seriously not capable of caring for this kitten for a couple of days, then fine. I'll find another home for him, even if I take half the night. Is that what you're saying?"

Braden's mouth opened, but he said nothing for a long time. "No," he finally admitted with reluctance. "I'm sure I can manage. What am I meant to feed him?"

"I've left you two days' worth of cans. If he goes through those, there are more at the supermarket."

"Wait! He needs to be fed every day?"

Marjorie was about to explain, then caught the glint of amusement in Braden's eyes. "Hilarious. I'll email you a list of things he shouldn't eat even though he'll try." She leaned in for a kiss then walked to the door. "And I'll call you tonight to make sure you haven't killed each other yet."

"Hm. Fancy a spot of zombie hunting?" Braden asked Shadow, lifting a controller in the air. "I've got one spare if you think you can add anything to the game."

As Marjorie closed the door, she heard Braden settling his new charge in front of the oversized TV. She listened for a while longer, smiling, then got into the car.

DESPITE HOW SHE'D assured Braden the kitten wouldn't come to any harm, Marjorie woke a few times during the night, her mind racing with all the things that could go wrong. A hairball might block Shadow's airway. The scratch from Monkey Business could become infected.

At midnight, just as she convinced herself it was perfectly normal to call Braden to make sure everything was fine, he sent her a text message. A picture of him holding Shadow and giving her a thumbs-up sign. With a sigh of relief, Marjorie lay back and promptly fell asleep.

Sunday, being her shortest trading day of the week, offered her and Esme another good stint of selling door to door. Unfortunately, the farther away they strayed from the village centre, the fewer houses they found occupied. Maybe leaving Monkey Business at home had tipped their luck.

"Oh, smell the pine," Esme enthused as they struck out at the tenth house in a row. "Perhaps we should give this up and walk back via the forest trails. I'm starting to think everybody's absconded for the holiday."

"I doubt the trolley would appreciate the dirt and pine needles but if you want to go that way, I'll meet you back at home."

"No way am I splitting up. I've seen too many horror movies to think that's ever a good idea."

"You think selling door to door is a horror movie?"

"It could be. All we need is a mad doctor lurking behind one of these doors and BOOM! We're in trouble."

A fantail landed on a large kowhai in front of them, its tail flashing and bobbing as it jerked around, trying to look in all directions at once. The two women came to a halt as they both watched the display. The bird launched itself towards a small cloud of midges: twisting, turning, stopping in mid-air then swooping back to regain its place on the branch.

As it darted off in search of a new target for its early evening meal, Marjorie sighed and gave the trolley a push. It stuck on a small divot in the footpath and when she shoved it harder, the wheel buckled underneath.

"Oh, no." She bent over to examine the damage, giving it a cautious kick in case that put everything to rights. "I'll need a wrench and a screwdriver to put it back in place."

Esme patted her pockets. "Pity. I don't have one on me. Can we just drag it home?"

"We'd need to lift it up." Marjorie picked

up the unwieldy object and managed a few steps. "I should've just brought a backpack."

"It's too late now for that kind of clever thinking." Esme bent over to examine the wheel in closer focus. "Can you balance it on one side?"

"Not for long." Marjorie took a step back and scanned the surrounding properties. They hadn't had much luck with door knocking when they were trying to sell but perhaps some reticent homeowners were lurking, ready to come forth to do a good deed.

"I can jog home and get Jerry to come back with the car."

"We can both do that," Marjorie said with a smile. "I doubt any thieves operating in Hanmer Springs are about to steal a broken trolley."

"But the biscuits?"

"Didn't you just say we shouldn't split up? Would you really leave me out here for the crazed doctor to attack?" Marjorie laughed to show she was joking, then headed across the road when she saw a curtain twitch. "I'll just ask in here if they've got some spare tools. If we strike out, then we can abandon the biscuits along with the trolley. I can bet which one is more likely not to be here when we come back."

When her first knock on the door failed to rouse anybody, Marjorie wondered if the curtain had been moved by a breeze or an open window. She tried again, this time hearing a shuffle of feet in response.

"Hey, there," she said in greeting, then faltered to a stop. "Jon? I didn't know you lived around here."

The young man's eyes widened at the sight of her. He closed the door an inch, then sighed and opened it back up. "I don't. Not usually. I'm just spending the night with some friends."

"I wondered if you had some tools. My trolley broke down across the road and I just need to get the wheel back into alignment."

"The community centre van's parked around the corner," Jon said, pointing down the long driveway. "I don't have tools here, but I can give you a lift home."

"That'd be great. Are you allowed to have the van overnight?"

The young man blew out a breath. "I'm looking forward to the day when I can have a conversation without someone second-guessing everything."

"Fair enough," Marjorie said, holding her hands up. "I take it back. You can use the van for whatever you want."

"Allie knows I've got it. Just a sec."

Jon disappeared inside and, after a moment, the door swung further inward, revealing a long hallway with several rooms leading off either side. Right at the end, a startled face stared back at her—a man with a large gift box in his hands. After jerking back, he kicked the door shut.

Marjorie turned and stared hard at the ground behind her. There was nothing suspicious about the situation. Any house still occupied would probably have at least a couple of presents inside, waiting for Christmas morning.

She could always ask Jon about it, then shook her head. Yeah. If he didn't like her asking about the van, he was hardly likely to volunteer information about the missing presents.

"It's probably a coincidence," she said firmly, rubbing at her eyebrow when it twitched.

"Talking to yourself, eh?" Jon said, coming outside and shutting the door. "It's the first sign of madness."

"It's the only way I can be sure of a decent conversation," Marjorie quipped back. "My friend's just waiting across the road. I'll go tell her you've offered us a lift."

While walking alongside the house on her way back to Esme, she couldn't resist a quick glance in the side windows. In the front room, the same man Marjorie had seen along the hallway was standing next to a large stack of boxes.

Boxes that could have held anything. Including the missing Christmas presents from the community centre.

CHAPTER TEN

"One, two, three, lift!" The trio swung the trolley up into the back of the van, nearly coming unstuck when the bent wheel caught on the floor.

"I've got it," Jon shouted as they struggled to keep the momentum going. Although the trolley had been light and manoeuvrable on the ground, it turned unwieldy as soon as its wheels parted company with the footpath.

With a final grunt of effort, it was far enough inside for the young man to slam the door closed. Esme ran a hand through her hair, instantly transforming into her usual immaculate self. Marjorie put her fingers up to her own greying ginger frizz and decided to leave well enough alone.

"Thanks for doing this," Esme said, jumping into the middle of the front bench seat and scrabbling for the lap belt. "It saves us a lot of trouble."

"No problem." Jon issued a wide grin. "Since I've got the loan of the community centre van, it's just as well I use it for helping members of the community."

Marjorie kept silent as she slid onto the seat. The stack of gifts she'd seen in the front room weighed heavily on her mind. Should she say something? Level an accusation? Or should she keep quiet and perhaps leave a crime undiscovered and unpunished?

She bit her lip and stared straight ahead, ignoring the worried sideways glance from her friend.

"Do you mind if we pop by the supermarket first?" Jon asked, clambering into the driver's seat. "Only, I promised my mates

I'd pick up dinner since they're helping me out with something."

"It'd be great," Esme enthused with a bright smile, perhaps to make up for Marjorie's silence. "There's a lovely pile of fresh vegetables waiting at home to be turned into a salad whereas my stomach is insisting on something far less healthy."

When Esme elbowed her in the side, Marjorie forced a smile. "It'd give me a chance to pick up a few cans of cat food. Braden looked terrified at the prospect of housing Shadow, so it'll give me an excuse to check on him."

"It's my worst fear," Esme said as her body relaxed into the seat. "You walking up to my door with a kitten who needs emergency housing."

Marjorie laughed. "Yes, you've mentioned that once or twice. Why do you think I chose Braden?"

"Does that happen often?" Jon glanced across, then returned his eyes to the road. "It sounds like a treat rather than a fear. I'd love a kitten to play with for a few days or weeks until he moves on to his forever home."

"Take a note," Esme said, giggling. "Quick! Before he takes it back."

"Do you keep a list?" Jon glanced at her again. "Because if so, definitely add my name to it."

"It's a big responsibility," Marjorie said, hedging. "And it almost never happens. If the kittens don't agree with a new addition, they go to another home. This situation is different since the police expect him to be with me."

Jon gave a gasp. "Why are the police involved with a kitten? What on earth did the little fellow do?"

His astonishment melted through Marjorie's reserve until she giggled. "Wrong place, wrong time."

There was no parking available in front of the supermarket, so Jon steered the vehicle around the corner. Just as they passed by the community centre, Marjorie caught a flash of movement from the corner of her eye and turned to see a man's legs disappearing through a window. "Stop!"

Nervous driver that he was, Jon slammed on the brakes so the seatbelt cut into her shoulder. Once she got her breath back, Marjorie jumped out of the car and took off running. Although she didn't waste time on explanations, Esme soon followed.

"Allie? Are you here?"

She tried the front door handle, but it was locked. Of course. Who would bother to break in through a window if they could just stroll through the front door?

"What did you see?"

Marjorie pointed at the open window while she felt along the top of the doorframe for a spare key. Perhaps the burglary had taught Allie better because she struck out. Luckily, Jon jogged up to join them a moment later, jingling a keyring.

"Stand aside. I've got this." He unlocked the door and ploughed inside without stopping to find out what 'this' was.

Marjorie followed hard on his heels.

"Whoever's in here, there's three of us and I'm about to call the police!"

"Already on it," Esme muttered, flashing her phone screen.

"Come out with your hands up," Jon shouted, as though he'd never been on the wrong side of the law.

A figure emerged from the side room with his hands in the air and a sheepish smile on his face. Evan Westcott.

"You!" Jon's hands clenched into fists. "Wasn't it enough to vandalise the centre? You thought you'd come back for another go?"

"I just want to visit with my son," the man called out, a tear dribbling down the side of his face. "That's all I've ever wanted."

"Breaking and entering isn't the way to gain custody." Marjorie glanced at Esme, who mouthed, *"They're on their way."*

"Neither is being the best parent I can be or jumping through every hoop the department has slung in front of me."

"Be quiet and lie on the floor," Jon ordered. "I don't want you darting off somewhere to cause more mischief. It took me six hours over two days to repair the last lot of damage you did."

"Were you the one who stole the Christmas presents?" Esme asked, walking over as the man followed Jon's instructions. "Did you think robbing the foster kids of a decent Christmas would be good fun?"

"What?" The puzzled expression had Marjorie half convinced he was innocent, then his lower lip pooched out like a spoiled brat. "I know nothing about that."

"A likely story." Esme crossed to the window and lifted the net curtains for a better view of the car park. "Either way, you can tell it all to the police. They're here."

Regina entered the centre gingerly with one hand on her Taser.

"Sorry," Esme called out. "I might have exaggerated the danger." She gave the prone man a light kick with her foot. "He's over here, looking far less threatening than he did originally."

"Mr Westcott," Regina said in a tired voice.

"Didn't I tell you to stay clear of the community centre? It's part of your bail condition."

She walked over and snapped a pair of straight cuffs on him, helping him to his feet. "The judge won't look favourably upon continued disturbances when she's already been lenient with your sentencing."

"I'll continue to fight until I gain custody of my son!"

"Your son doesn't live at the community centre," the officer retorted. "They're just trying to do their best to run a place for the townsfolk to enjoy, you included. This isn't the right way to repay the thankless job it is to keep the centre open. Nor will it do you any good in your fight to regain custody."

At the door, she turned back to the group. "It'll help if you can all come down to the station right now if that's possible. I'd like to get this arrest filed away before my end of shift."

"We weren't doing anything else," Esme said, hurrying out the door.

Jon trailed along with more reluctance and Marjorie gave a shrug. "I suppose it beats door knocking."

The station was busy for a Sunday with only two chairs in the waiting room available. At their surprised expressions, Regina explained, "It always gets like this around Christmas. Just wait till next week where we have half a dozen families who turn a minor disagreement over the table into a physical altercation."

Jon stood, his back so ramrod straight that Marjorie doubted he would have sat even if space had been available. Esme stared around with an alert expression, obviously enjoying the novelty.

"Do you think they're any closer to finding out who murdered Martin?" she asked in such a loud whisper Marjorie felt confident everyone in the building heard.

"I don't know and it's not really any of our business."

"But should we tell them what his ex-wife and neighbour told us?"

"That they didn't do it?" Marjorie asked with a chuckle. "I'm sure they've already told the police that a dozen times over."

When Regina called her into an interview room, there were purplish-grey circles underneath her eyes.

"Haven't you been getting enough sleep?"

The officer shook her head. "I haven't been getting enough anything. No offence to anyone who loves this time of year, but I wish the festive season was over. It'd be nice to enjoy the summer without all the stress and weirdness the holidays bring."

It had been a long time since Christmas meant anything to Marjorie except two days with the café closed, but the holiday was still deeply entwined with memories of church in the morning, followed by presents, then the biggest meal of the year. Even if those things no longer happened, the emotions they stirred up gave her a warm glow.

The warmth appeared to be missing from the rest of Hanmer Springs.

"What did you want to know?"

They quickly ran through the events of the break in and Marjorie shifted in the wooden chair, feeling her skirt clinging to the backs of her legs in the heat. "Doesn't the government budget stretch to air conditioning?"

"It's broken. This place is so old half of it's stopped working."

The first flat Marjorie had stayed in after the breakdown of her marriage had been like that. She remembered sitting on the floor, howling after a light switch shorted the electricity and the chair she sat on to recover from the shock broke. "Maybe you should ask for a new unit from Santa."

Regina rolled her eyes and glanced over her scrawled notes. The entire interview was being recorded but Marjorie had noticed her friend liked to do things the old-fashioned way. "Where were you coming from?"

"Farther up the road from my place, probably an hour's walk." She tried to think of the last number she'd seen and only managed to ignite a small pulse in the back of her eyes.

"Near the camping ground?"

"Other way." Marjorie snapped her finger as the letterbox from Jon's place spun into her mind. "Two seventy-five. I saw someone was home, and it was plain luck to find Jon there with a van. I had no idea he lived that far out of town."

"Jon Roscoe?"

Judging from the tight set of Regina's mouth, Marjorie thought she'd said something wrong. "Yes," she drawled. "That's right."

Regina slammed her palm flat on the table. "The idiot. That's the place his old gang hangs out. As if they haven't got him in enough trouble roping him into being their getaway driver, now he's messing about with them again."

Marjorie felt like a miserable snitch as she opened her mouth again. "That's not all. I saw a pile of boxes in the front room of the property. There's a good chance they're the ones who stole the Christmas presents."

CHAPTER ELEVEN

When the two women came back into the station waiting room, Marjorie couldn't raise her eyes from the ground. Even if she'd done nothing more than tell the truth, her twisting stomach insisted her statement was vile.

"Jon Roscoe? I'll see you next," Regina said, shuffling him along the corridor towards the interview room without giving a single thing away.

"Was the questioning that bad?" Esme asked in surprise, then when Marjorie shook her head, "Why the long face?"

"I saw a whole pile of gifts in the front room of Jon's place when I was walking along the driveway," Marjorie admitted, close to tears. "Apparently, the house belongs to a gang."

"Pfft. Not your fault if you saw something." Esme leaned over to pat Marjorie on the knee. "My mouth is as loose as an oiled hinge so you can bet if I'd seen something, I'd spill the beans, too."

"I just wish the wheel hadn't broken, and we'd gone straight home."

"In which case, that dreadful man would've broken into the community centre unseen and might've caused all kinds of damage. No matter how much sympathy I have with Evan over missing his son, there's no call for his bad behaviour."

The thought cheered Marjorie a little until Jon came back into the front of the station, his hands balled into fists. Regina's jaw was clenched so hard it could have been carved from marble.

"Was it you that made up all those lies?"

Jon asked, jerking his chin angrily at Marjorie. "I had nothing to do with robbing those presents!"

"Then the whole matter should sort itself out soon," Esme said, fixing him with a hard stare. "And my friend doesn't lie."

"Come on," Regina said, pulling at Jon's elbow. "Show me what you're talking about."

"Why? So you can nick all my friends?"

"Nobody is arresting anyone without evidence. If your friends weren't involved with the burglary, then you've got nothing to worry about."

"I've watched enough about Teina Pora to know different."

"How about you stop with the drama? I can either drive you back to the property and park out on the street, or I can pull up the driveway, lights flashing."

Jon's face blanched. "Can't I drive you in the van?"

Regina snorted with amusement. "No, you can't. I need to come back to work afterwards."

"Then I've no way of getting home again."

"That place isn't your home."

The two glared at each other, neither relenting until Marjorie cleared her throat. "How about I take the van keys and drop off the broken trolley before meeting you at the house? Then I can take you for a ride back to your actual home."

"There you go," Regina said, pulling on Jon's arm again. "Sorted. Throw the lady the keys."

It was a short detour to check on the kittens and store the trolley in the back of the café, then Marjorie and Esme hit the road, retracing their afternoon journey. Regina's police car sat a few houses along from the property, which must mean Jon was behaving.

Esme peered in the front window as Marjorie inched the van up the long driveway. "I see what you mean," she said in a cold voice. "That looks exactly like what was taken from the centre."

They knocked and Regina answered the

door. "Come inside. Jon's got a rather interesting story."

Marjorie followed Esme into the lounge room, cupping her elbows. Jon sat on the sofa with a serious case of man-spread while two of his friends sat in recliners, waiting impatiently to return to their game.

"I felt bad about the kids missing out on their Christmas," Jon said in a small voice, rubbing the back of his neck. "When I first found out about the party, I thought they were being spoiled rotten. I had nothing like that when I was a kid. Then the presents were stolen, and I couldn't stop picturing how disappointed they'd be." He cleared his throat as his voice thickened. "Perhaps if I had something nice like the party happen when I was younger, I would've turned out better."

"You turned out alright, mate," one friend said from his chair. "And it's them should apologise for accusing you of stuff you didn't do!"

"I've done enough in the past," Jon said, cracking his knuckles. "Anyway, I had a think after hearing about the burglary and worked out I had enough in my savings to pay for a few replacement toys. I came around here to borrow the last few dollars I needed, and my mates decided they could contribute something too."

"They've been canvassing everyone in town, raising funds for the presents," Regina said, beaming with pride as though Jon were her son. "The gifts in the front room are donated goods or stuff they've raised the money to buy."

A blush started at the neckline of Marjorie's blouse, creeping steadily upwards until her entire face was bright crimson. "I should never have mentioned anything. I'm so sorry."

"No need to apologise," Regina said, though Jon's face suggested he might have different thoughts on the matter. "And Jon knows full well it's against the spirit of his sentence to be associating with these friends."

The two young men in question shot her

guilty grins before hunching lower in their recliners.

"You've had the same idea as us," Esme said, clapping her hands together and beaming a smile at Jon. "Marjorie and I have been going door to door, selling biscuits and massages to afford to replace the presents. We should pool our resources and see how far we've still got to go."

While Regina waved goodbye and backed out of the house, Esme and Jon eagerly set to work comparing lists and figures. After a phone call to Nigel to get an update on the fundraising page, Esme exclaimed, "But this is fantastic. We're halfway there."

"Only halfway?" Jon tugged at his ear, a worried expression on his face. "We've only got a few days left and I don't know who else to call on."

"What more do we need?" Marjorie asked, leaning over to squint at the totals. "I know someone who might help."

SIX OF THEM gathered at the Skinner residence. Jon and his two friends had insisted on coming, plus Esme and Marjorie, with Nigel driving to meet them there.

"I don't think we all had to come out," Marjorie said with a nervous laugh. "We might just scare them."

"Oh, yeah." Esme hooked up an eyebrow, scanning the motley crew. "We're ferocious-looking, alright."

"Just knock on the door," Nigel said, switching his weight from one foot to another. "If you don't do it soon, I'll take over."

Marjorie pressed the doorbell and stood back as a long tune played. When it died away, she could hear the clip of high heels coming along the hallway.

"Lillian," she said warmly, taking a step forward and holding out her hand. "I don't know if you remember me…"

"Marjorie." Mrs Skinner peered over her shoulder and the wide smile faltered. "How can I help you?"

"Did you hear about the burglary at the community centre?" When the woman's eyes widened in shock, Marjorie continued, "Well, we're hoping you and your husband might help us out."

"Claude?" Lillian backed away from the door, turning and shouting for her husband again, "Claude, there's somebody here to see you."

When he arrived at the door, he had a polite but puzzled expression on his face. "What's this about?"

"I wondered if you'd heard about the Christmas present theft from the community centre?" Marjorie turned to the group, and they grew appropriately sad-eyed. "We're fundraising to replace the items lost in the burglary."

"Haven't I donated to that already?" Claude asked, raising his eyebrows at his wife, who nodded. "I'm not made of money, you know."

"We realise it's a tough time for many people. That's why we wanted to do something special for a benefactor who could take us to the goal." Marjorie held up her hands, miming a headline. "The Claude Skinner Community Christmas Party. We'd name the whole shebang in your honour."

"You would?" He stroked his chin and stared at the floor for a second.

"It sounds like a lovely way to be honoured by the community," Lillian hastened to say, stepping forward. "Would there be a banner?"

Marjorie gulped and shot a panicked expression at the team.

"Obviously," Nigel stepped forward, grabbing hold of Mrs Skinner's hands and clutching them tightly. "It would make a wonderful keepsake. And we'd make sure the local press got a good selection of photographs for the paper. We'd take the best shot and frame it as a token of thanks for your generosity."

"Can we really do that?" Esme whispered, looking doubtful.

Nigel gave a last pump of Lillian's hands and stepped back. "We can do a rush job through the local printers," he whispered to Esme. "Manny owes me a few favours."

"What security would there be at the community centre?" Claude asked. "Only, I'd heard some items had gone missing even before the burglary."

"What? Where did you hear that?" Esme squeaked while Marjorie stepped forward.

"Jon will provide security around the clock until the party is over," she said, winking at the young man. "He'll be camped out on the sofa in the room where the presents will be kept."

When Claude continued to stare at his wife, undecided, Marjorie wrote the required figure and showed the page to the couple. "This is the amount we're seeking."

Lillian frowned, but not at the total. She bit her lower lip and crossed her arms over her stomach. "Was there more than one theft?"

Marjorie was pleased to see their entire group appeared confused. She didn't understand the question herself but readily answered, "Not that we've heard of. The gifts all appeared to be taken on the same night, by the same culprits."

"Perhaps someone at the centre got light-fingered and helped themselves before the burglary?" Claude suggested, then shrugged. "I'm sure we've all known light-fingered employees."

"Nobody from the community centre took anything!" Jon said with his face burning. "Allie and I are there most of the time and the rest of the volunteers are honest people." He stepped forward, poking Claude in the chest. "Or would you like to accuse me to my face?"

"I'm sure Mr Skinner didn't—"

"Get off my property," Claude said with a sniff. "I've already contributed to the party once and I don't see why I should be harassed into donating again."

He slammed the door.

"Merry Christmas," Esme said and burst into tears.

CHAPTER TWELVE

*D*espite their experience at the Skinner's residence, everyone in the group agreed to meet the next day and work out the next steps to raise the last of the money.

"Is there any chance the donation page will take off overnight?" Marjorie asked Nigel with crossed fingers, but he shook his head.

"I've advertised it as far as I can without spending more money than we'd be making. Unless a notable influencer picks it up out of the blue, it'll just trickle in the same way it has been."

That night, instead of slumping in front of the television, Marjorie opened her laptop and went onto various social media pages. Influencers should live there somewhere, shouldn't they?

If they did, Marjorie didn't know how to track them down. She made new accounts on sites she hadn't bothered with in the past and followed the people a quick search told her might be helpful. How a person went from a follower to asking for the person to send out a message, she didn't know.

"I'm the wrong generation for this lark," she told Monkey Business as he curled up next to her. He opened his eyes and mouth wide, tongue lolling out. The gesture made her laugh, but it didn't get her any closer to an idea.

As if trying to distract her, Toil and Trouble pushed an assortment of unread magazines off the coffee table. When she picked them up and scolded the kittens, they responded with chastened expressions, doing exactly the same again as soon as she settled on the couch.

"I don't know whether to indulge you or lock you up," she said, wrinkling her nose at the pair. "But so long as you stick with paper, I'm happy."

They had little chance for anything else upstairs. After years of cohabitation with kittens, Marjorie had either fastened items securely on tabletops or wouldn't weep over their demise.

"While I'm on here, I should check in with the breeder of your nemesis and see if she has another buyer lined up who'd take Shadow."

Monkey Business feigned innocence at the name but stared intently at the screen as Marjorie searched through social media for the woman and gave a cry of triumph when she found her.

"Now, if I'm still sitting here watching videos in another hour, give me a poke," she instructed the chocolate Persian before pressing play on a display of Lykoi kitten adorability. From there, she read an article about the new breed.

Although she checked through every recent post on the page and followed links off-site into uncharted internet waters, Marjorie couldn't find any information about potential buyers. If they had expressed an interest on the page, they must have been directed to a private message conversation. Either that, or there was no interest at all, which seemed unlikely given the amount of likes each post attracted.

"It looks like I'll have to send her a message," Marjorie said while giving Monkey a cuddle. "Fingers crossed she checks her other folder."

With the enquiry sent, she promptly played every video linked to the page again. "Just to be thorough," she explained when the Persian yawned.

With her curiosity sated, Marjorie sent a quick text to Braden to assure herself the real kitten was doing just as well as the videoed ones. An image was sent back to her—

Braden with the Lykoi perched on his head. Not the recommended position for a cuddle but the two of them seemed to be getting on well.

"Oh, I'm an idiot," she exclaimed as she got under the bedcovers. "I went to all that trouble to persuade Claude Skinner to donate and overlooked the developer with bulging pockets who I'm in business with."

Leaving a reminder for the morning to harangue Shaun Hayes until he coughed up at least something towards the replacement gifts, Marjorie fell asleep with a smile on her face.

"BUT YOU HAVE TO COME ALONG," Esme pleaded as Marjorie set up her café for opening. "If you're not there, Shaun will have no problem turning us down flat."

"No, he won't." At her friend's pouting expression, Marjorie laughed and pinched her cheek. "I can give you a handwritten letter begging for the money if you like, but I need to get this place open."

"I can look after the café." Esme grabbed an apron off the stack and picked Toil off a nearby tabletop before he could consign the printed menu to the floor. She wasn't quick enough to save the neighbouring table where Trouble was showing off his talents. "You know I've got this in hand. I watch the place for you often enough when you need something."

The statement might just have been part of her arsenal to manipulate Marjorie into doing what she wanted, but it worked well because it was true. A year before, they'd probably shared their responsibilities to monitor each other's businesses equally but in the past six or seven months, Marjorie had used the service a lot more than the masseuse had.

"Okay. You get to play with the kittens while I beg for money from my business partner." Marjorie unwound her apron and gave Monkey Business a pat.

"Well, you don't have to go yet," Esme

protested as a tourist van pulled up outside. "He won't be at work until ten at the earliest."

Marjorie hesitated long enough for her friend's eyes to grow panicked, then relented. "I'll wait until after the morning tea rush." She tied the apron back on again as a dozen customers wandered through the front doors.

It was a surprisingly busy day with enough people dropping by to make it worth opening. Just as Marjorie thought she'd have a decent chance to abscond and meet with Shaun, Lillian Skinner walked inside, clutching her purse chain as though defending it against a mugger.

Marjorie pulled a face at Esme, then turned a bright smile on the unexpected guest. "What would you like?"

"Is there somewhere we can chat for a moment?" Lillian glanced over her shoulder with a posture so stiff she appeared robotic.

"Sure, grab the table in the corner," Marjorie said, pointing to one with no occupied neighbours nearby. "I'll bring along a couple of coffees."

"You mightn't need to make that trip after all," Esme whispered. "Now go sit beside her and I'll deal with the drinks."

Marjorie sat opposite Lillian, relaxing her muscles in direct proportion to the stiffness in the other woman. As Toil and Trouble dashed over, she plucked them up, one in each hand, and passed one kitten across while keeping the other in her lap.

"Oh, I shouldn't..." Mrs Skinner held her hands up to either side while the black kitten sniffed at her suit jacket with curiosity. It was warm enough outside already to make the extra layer redundant, but Marjorie surmised the woman probably wore it no matter how hot the day.

"It's what the kittens are here for," she said, laughing as Trouble launched himself up her chest to pad his oversized paws on her shoulder. "If you're worried about hairs on your clothing, I've got a stock of lint rollers by the door."

Lillian gave the kitten a cautious pat, then became more involved as Toil reacted to her strokes. "My son would love this place," she said with a long sigh. "Claude doesn't believe in keeping pets, but Toby wants to adopt every animal he sees."

"How old is Toby again?"

"He just turned fourteen a month ago and has become quite the little adult." Lillian smiled for the first time since entering the café. "We bought him a suit for a school play he had the lead role for and when he puts it on, he's like a mini-me version of Claude. It's adorable."

"Bring him by if you think he'd like the kittens." Marjorie broke off into a set of giggles as Trouble nosed around the back of her neck. "We don't get many children here but he's more than welcome."

"I'll mention it. With the school holidays, I'm finding it hard to keep him occupied all day."

Esme brought over the coffees and, seeing there was no one needing a refill, sat with them. "What did you come in here for? Did your husband reconsider the donation?"

"Oh, no." Lillian's shoulder hunched, and she blushed a deep crimson. "Sorry to mislead you, if that's what you thought. No, I came here because I've made a silly mistake."

She took a sip of coffee, then drained the cup. Marjorie sat back, repositioning Trouble and letting the woman speak in her own time.

"Those gifts I brought to the community centre," she finally said in a halting voice. "I accidentally picked up a box that shouldn't have been included."

"Oh my goodness. And now they've been stolen!" Marjorie leaned over to pat Lillian's forearm. "I'm so sorry."

"It's just..." The woman broke off as a tear rolled down her face. "I thought there might be a chance it was still at the centre. You see, it was an unsealed box, and the contents didn't match the outside..."

Marjorie nodded. "If that's true, it wouldn't have been wrapped and placed with the others. From what Allie told me, there are some checks that every donated present goes through and if they don't pass, they don't go under the tree."

Lillian's eyes brightened. "So the mistaken box might still be at the community centre?"

"It could be." Marjorie frowned, trying to remember if Allie or the others had mentioned what they did with the rejects. She didn't want to bother the woman if the information was available elsewhere. From what she'd seen, Allie was skating close to the edge of her endurance for nonsense. "Felix, Dotty, and Braden were the ones dealing with the gift collection and wrapping," she said with a snap of her fingers. "I'll call Braden and see if he knows where the box is now."

But when she dialled his number, it went straight to voicemail. "I'll leave a message and get back to you when he replies. What did the box look like?"

"Hm?"

"If you give me a description, I'll get Braden to bring it around to you or pick it up myself."

"Gosh, no." Lillian seemed appalled at the

idea. "I'm not having people running all over town to correct my mistake. If he tells me where it's likely to be, I'll sort it out from there." She deposited Toil on the floor and stood up, opening her purse. "How much for the coffee?"

"On the house," Marjorie said at the same time Esme quoted the price. "You really don't have to—"

"I can afford to pay," Lillian said, passing over a far higher bill than was needed. "And if you don't want to take it, you can put it towards the replacement Christmas present fund."

"Deal," Esme said, snatching up the money as though afraid Marjorie would open her mouth again and make it disappear.

CHAPTER THIRTEEN

"I have to say, I'm insulted." Shaun Hayes leaned back in his chair, swivelling to one side so he could stare out the window. "There's almost no one left in the business district this week except for me, yet you still found another man to approach first."

"We were saving the best for last," Marjorie said, hoping her act of enthusiasm would cover her embarrassment. "And I only thought of Claude Skinner first because I'd helped his wife haul her donated gifts into the community centre a few days ago."

"I have a good mind to decline the offer because of it."

Her shoulders sagged and Marjorie suddenly felt like weeping. After Shaun, she had no ideas left and going door to door wouldn't get them over the line in time.

"Jeez, I was just kidding," Shaun said in a concerned voice as her head dropped. "Have a tissue."

He pushed a box across the table and Marjorie blew her nose. "Sorry. It's been a rough couple of days."

"I'm not surprised. The entire community is upended when something like this happens. I used to think this was a safe town."

"Me too." Marjorie pushed her frizzy hair out of her eyes. "Even with people starting to rally around, everything feels off-kilter."

Shaun gave an unexpected laugh. "Look at that!" He pointed out the window. "I take it back."

Jon and his friends had set up a mat in the middle of the paved area in the park. While a small pair of speakers blared music, he dropped to the ground and started to breakdance.

"Who'd have thought that style would come back," Shaun said, shaking his head. "I used to try that myself during the eighties."

"Really?" Marjorie stood up and moved to the window for a closer look. "Were you any good?"

"Come on." Shaun clapped his hands together and held open the office door for her to exit. "Let's see exactly how many moves this old dinosaur has left in him."

Marjorie flashed an astonished expression at the secretary as she passed by, gesturing for her to follow along. Part of her thought it was a joke until Shaun crossed the street and held up a hand in greeting to the small group that was assembling. "Allow me to demonstrate the old-school methods. Anyone care to pay for a request?"

A couple who'd stopped to watch burst out laughing and tossed a handful of gold coins into the hat positioned in front of the mat. "How about a windmill?" the woman asked, clutching onto her partner's arm in excitement. "Bonus points if you make it through without breaking a hip."

The receptionist burst into laughter as her boss dropped to the mat and began to gyrate his legs out, letting the momentum swing him from one angle to the next. He stopped with his legs straight out, ankles crossed together, posing up on one elbow. An ending that was greeted with much applause.

"Head spin," a new arrival called out, clapping in time to the music. Marjorie looked on in wonder as Shaun made it through the move alive and cupped a hand around his ear in anticipation for the next shouted request.

"Is he your business partner?" Jon asked, coming to stand beside Marjorie. "Because the old dude's got some sweet moves."

"He is. I was halfway through asking him for the rest of the money when he saw you." She stopped and gasped as Shaun jackhammered, her wrist aching in sympathy.

"I had no idea he planned on raising it this way."

Shaun jumped to his feet, moving to the edge of the mat and waving Jon's mates onto centre stage. "I'd better let you guys take over. Don't want to show you up." As the new dancers broke out their moves, he leaned over to Marjorie and whispered, "I think my body just reminded my head it's not as young as it thinks it is."

"You did well," Jon said in admiration, holding out his hand to shake. "If my old man tried something like that, he'd be on his way to hospital by now."

"Is this fundraising for the Christmas party?" Shaun jerked his head at the cap now filling rapidly with coins. "Because I'm happy to hand over my credit card to top up the balance if you've got someone ready to buy the presents."

"Thank you," Marjorie cried, giving him a kiss on the cheek. "That's wonderful."

"We're happy to do the shopping," Jon said with a grin. "And we've got Felix lined up to help with the wrapping." He dropped his voice to a whisper. "Me and my mates tried but they don't exactly look professional."

"I'm sure the children won't mind," Marjorie whispered back.

Her phone vibrated, and she pulled it out to see an image of Braden and Shadow on the floor, bums in the air, eating—or pretending to eat—from food bowls. With a snort, Marjorie dialled his number. "It looks like you found something in common."

"I'll bond with anyone over food and he's turned into a dab hand at the controller."

"Oh, yeah?"

"Mm-hm. He also dispatched a particularly nasty zombie attack by crawling over the remote."

She quickly interpreted the sentence in her head. "He turned off the TV screen?"

"That's the one. I'm afraid to turn it back on and see the damage."

"Did you see my message?"

"Yeah. Felix and Dotty took care of all that. I think they've stashed the rejected presents in their spare room until after the party. They were going to go through them with a fine-tooth comb later and I offered to auction them off since I'm doing the electronics, anyway."

"So there's a chance the missing box will be in their house?"

"A good chance. They were rigorous about sorting the gifts when I went out collecting with them. I can still see the heartbroken face of Carly Mann when Dotty tore off her beautiful wrapping paper to ensure the item inside really was a doll."

"Ouch." Despite knowing the reasons, Marjorie winced. "And we've got an update on the donations."

"Shaun came through?"

"With flying colours. Just a moment…" She waved Shaun back onto the dance mat and took a quick photograph. "He earned extra through unexpected means."

Braden chuckled. "We should make sure that image takes the front cover of the next community newspaper. It's a keeper."

"I'll pass on your appreciation."

She hung up, smiling, and tried to dial Lillian's number. "Does nobody have their phones turned on anymore," she grumbled as it hit the woman's voicemail and she had to send a text message instead.

Just as she finished, her phone vibrated again, this time with a social media notification. A message flashed up on the screen from the Lykoi breeder. *I remember Shadow and have the name of another person who had an interest in purchasing him.*

"Yay," she said, raising eyebrows from Shaun and Jon. "It's kitten business, not Christmas business." Marjorie moved to a seat and began to type a message into her phone with awkward thumbs.

"I'd love to have the second name. Unfortunately, the owner died and we're looking to rehouse the kitten."

A shocked emoji came back, followed a moment later by another message.

"The other interested party was Martin Thorpe."

Marjorie stared at the screen with her brow furrowed. What was the polite way to say to a stranger, "You're wrong?"

"That's the name of the owner who died," she typed back. *"Who was the other person?"*

"Really? I sold Shadow to a man named Claude Skinner. I'd almost completed the transaction with Martin when Claude swooped in and paid double. Although I felt awful for selling the kitten out from under him, I couldn't pass up the offer."

Marjorie stared at the message for so long the screen darkened.

Martin owned a kitten paid for by Claude Skinner. A gift that at double the going rate must have cost him close to ten thousand.

She replaced the phone in her pocket, frowning into mid-air. Had Martin somehow stolen the kitten from Claude? No, that didn't make sense. She could hear Lillian's breathy voice in her ear. *"Claude doesn't believe in keeping pets."*

What on earth was going on?

"Come on," Jon shouted to her. "Don't you

KATHERINE HAYTON

want to come to Christchurch to pick out the new presents?"

Marjorie shook her head to clear it and smiled. "I'd love to, but I need to get back to the café. Do you have someone else to help?"

The two mates standing close by nodded vigorously, and she laughed. "Call me when you get back to town and I'll help with the wrapping."

Jon waved, jogging backwards towards the community centre van. "Will do!"

CHAPTER FOURTEEN

"I've been rushed off my feet," Esme declared when Marjorie made it back to the café. The masseuse wiped a hand over her brow with a theatrical flourish and sank into a chair.

The rest of the seats were empty and, judging by the tables' pristine surfaces, the last occupants were long gone. A few kittens were on their feet, playing, but the majority sagged in the corner, dozing.

"Yeah, it looks hectic," Marjorie said, flapping a teatowel at her friend. "Thank you for covering."

"I've paid myself out of your display case." Esme patted her stomach. "But if you want to sit and have a bite, I think there's room."

Marjorie made them each a coffee and piled a plate high with an assortment of scones, muffins, and biscuits. Once upon a time, she'd thought baking every day would soon cure her sugar addiction—a faint hope quickly banished.

"You missed a real sight in town," she said, queuing up the picture she'd taken of Shaun. "And Jon is en route to Christchurch with a list of goodies to collect and bring home. He might call us later. I offered to help with wrapping."

"That sounds like fun," Esme said, stifling a yawn on the back of her hand and propping her feet on another chair. "Honestly, unless your trade picks up, you should close this place tomorrow and come for a picnic with Jerry and me."

"Where are you going?"

"Dunno. The plan only just occurred to me." She pulled her phone out and started texting. "I suppose I should check if he's free before I offer his company as a drawcard."

"Don't worry on my account." Marjorie held up her hand. "I'm opening tomorrow. Between the busload this morning and my regulars who're expecting me to be here, it's a done deal."

"You're no fun."

"Why don't you drum up some massage appointments and we can have a nice normal working day?"

Esme stared at her as though she were crazy. "And, as I said, you're—"

"No fun," Marjorie finished for her. "Yeah, I got that."

"My client list always dries up in the middle of summer," Esme complained. "Who'd have thought people would prefer to spend the holidays with their friends or family rather than having me massage them in the stuffy studio?"

"Well, don't put that in your advertising, okay?"

Just as Marjorie considered pulling in her

sign early, a car pulled up outside, then another. "And you wanted me to close," she chided Esme as the afternoon rush picked up steam and the kittens awoke refreshed and full of mischief from their snoozes. "At this rate, I'll be lucky to shut on time."

Luckily, the patrons left with a few minutes to spare before her usual three o'clock finish. Although her phone had been dinging with messages, it wasn't until Marjorie had finished wiping down the tables and sorting the leftovers that she checked them.

Braden had invited her to take back her hellcat with a lovely shot of a leather sofa used as a scratching post and Jon had left a note that they'd collected the gifts and were meeting up at Felix's to pull everything together.

With a sympathetic shrug at the damage Shadow had inflicted, Marjorie sent a message back to Jon and walked across to tap on Esme's door.

"I think I'll pass up on the wonderful

opportunity," her friend said, gesturing towards her television where her streaming service wanted to know if she was still there. "Four episodes down, eight to go."

As Toil and Trouble double-teamed a tray of napkins off the main counter, Marjorie decided they'd do well to come along with her. "Be nice and cute and we'll see if we can rehouse you two before the night's done." Although she pulled out two pet carriers for the journey, the black felines eagerly squeezed into one.

"Thank goodness," Jon said, clapping his hands together as he showed her along the corridor to the main room—or bomb site to be more accurate. "A lady! Please teach us how to work magic with sticky tape and paper."

She laughed, thinking it was a joke, but Jon turned out to be serious. He ensconced her behind a large table, full of supplies, and insisted Marjorie give them lessons.

"Okay, but you'll need to keep hold of these two while I give a demonstration," she said, handing him Toil and depositing Trouble into Felix's startled arms. "First off, place the box in the centre of the paper. Fold over the leading edge to give it a sharp crease and tape it directly to the box, like so."

She took them through her process three times before they were let loose on the stack of gifts. "And for goodness' sake," Marjorie reminded them as a parcel was presented to her with no tag. "Add a note to say if it's for a boy or a girl and the age range. Santa will be cantankerous enough wearing a heavy red suit and beard in the middle of summer. Let's not make him any more upset by expecting him to mind-read."

Jon appeared quite taken with the idea of a grumpy Santa.

Braden sent her another message, this time with a tin of empty cat food in one hand and a floor covered in the contents in the other. "*Send help. Enemy combatant.*"

She texted back their address and invited him to come on over, bringing the kitten with him. When the breeder had informed her the other interested party was Claude

Skinner, a man who apparently didn't want a pet at all, she'd hoped Braden might bond with him and take away the need to rehouse Shadow.

Now he was acting up, she couldn't in good conscience leave them together. If Monkey Business's nose continued to be put out of joint by the small kitten, her next stop would probably be animal rescue.

Marjorie didn't like to pass animals their way, considering they worked with a strict time limit for rehousing pets, but she couldn't think of another option right now. Somebody in their community would surely see how cute Shadow was and adopt him.

"You've got a long face for someone wrapping presents," one of Jon's mates said. Marjorie hadn't concentrated when he reeled off everyone's names and now drew a blank. "Woody," the young man said in response to her blank stare. "And this is Jared."

"Nice to meet you. I'm just trying to sort out a new home for a kitten and it's causing a small headache."

"One of these?" Jared gestured to Toil and Trouble. "But they're adorable."

"I'm glad you think so. They also need to be rehoused but there's a particular one who's more trouble. He's not the prettiest kitten in the world and he seems to be upsetting the men in my life."

When Woody gave her a startled glance, Marjorie amended, "One of those men being my cat."

"I told you I could babysit a kitten if you needed help," Jon said, overhearing. "I'd take great care of him, I promise."

Marjorie felt a weight lift as she studied the young man, who was full of surprises. "I might need to take you up on that. Would it be okay with your parents?"

"Yeah. Mum won't even notice, and my stepdad loves cats."

She opened her mouth to thank him when she was interrupted by the sound of someone falling over in a side room. Marjorie's brow creased as Jon stared, Felix flinched, and Woody and Jared stood up, fists at the ready.

"There shouldn't be anyone else in here," Felix said in a worried tone. He dropped the parcel he was working on and lumbered to his feet with a groan. "I'd better go check it out."

"Not alone, you won't," Jon said as he and his mates flanked the older man.

"Should I call the police?" Marjorie asked, pulling her phone out. She saw the reply from Braden, saying he was on his way and hesitated. Could it be him? He might have missed the front door and crawled in through a window.

She shook her head at the idiocy of the thought just as Jon replied, "Let's see what we're dealing with first."

He stood by the door, waiting until everyone was grouped around it before he pulled the handle. A furious Claude Skinner sat on the floor, cradling his ankle.

"What on earth are you doing here?" Felix demanded. "This is private property."

"Yeah. I'm retrieving private property and all," Claude replied, then pulled a pistol out of his inside pocket when Felix took a step towards him. "Watch it there, old man. You don't want me to splatter your brains across the wall just before Christmas."

With shaking hands, Marjorie flicked her thumb across the mobile screen to wake it, then pressed the phone icon for the numbers to appear.

"Drop the phone, love. I don't want to shoot you either."

As she stared at the handgun, now aimed in her direction, the cell phone tumbled from her numb hands.

"Now, just give me a minute." Claude reached behind him for the edge of the single bed and heaved himself upright. "If this place wasn't in such a mess, I never would've tripped, so how about we pretend you didn't hear me."

"What are you doing here?" Marjorie asked. Her blood was now pounding through her temples with such force, she could barely hear her own voice.

"I came to collect something that's mine," he said as his eyes flicked to either side. "My wife added a box to the stack of presents, and I want it back, that's all."

"You stole the presents," she said, pulling Lillian and Claude's odd behaviour together in an answer that turned her stomach. "That's what you were talking about last night when you said some things had gone missing before the burglary. You stole those kid's presents from the community centre and couldn't find your silly box."

Claude raised his eyebrows. "Well done. Now, if you could show me where it is, I'd be grateful."

Marjorie turned to Felix, who appeared nonplussed. "He's talking about a box where the seal was broken, and the contents didn't match the outside. At least, that's what his wife told me."

"From the collections?" Felix raised his hands and backed up a step. "I've taken all of those over to Allie's. We did that on the afternoon before the burglary."

At the mention of the older woman, Marjorie felt a shot of pure fear rush through her body. She opened her mouth to protest, then worked through what Felix had said. "No, it would've been after that. Lillian brought the boxes directly to the community centre, right before closing. After you'd sorted out the collected presents."

Felix clicked his tongue and tipped his head to one side. "Okay, gotcha." His voice sounded relieved. "They're in the car. I had them in the lounge and Dotty growled that I was turning her best room for entertaining into an oversized storage locker, so I shoved them into the boot instead."

"Right, then," Claude said, stepping forward. "Show me."

Felix didn't budge. "Not with that weapon, I'm not. I'm happy to take you outside and show you what's there but I'm not doing it at gunpoint."

"Go out alone and bring it inside, then." Claude let his arms drop but didn't loosen the grip on the pistol. "I'll stay here with your friends. If you want to run, just remember them."

Felix's face hardened but Jon and his mates nodded. "Go on," Woody said. "The quicker you get it, the quicker this'll all be over."

As the older man left the room, Jon stared hard at Claude. "What's in the box, anyway?"

"None of your business."

"Better not be drugs. I've seen a lot of my friends ruin their lives because of that filth."

Claude rolled his eyes. "It's not drugs. Calm yourself."

As the minutes stretched out, the room seemed to grow closer. Marjorie cleared her throat. "How about we move into the lounge? There's not much space for us all in here."

"Good idea," Claude said, jerking the pistol in that direction. "It'll give me a better view of what your friend's up to."

When they moved back into the larger room, Marjorie shooed Toil and Trouble away from the gunman, scared their presence would irritate someone unused to pets.

"I've got what you want," a voice called from the corridor, definitely not belonging to

Felix. With a start of horror, Marjorie realised she knew who it was.

Braden.

"No," she called out, wanting to run along the hallway and push him out of the house. "It's not safe."

He turned into the room, smiling with the same easy charm he had when explaining why it was important to spend hours every day, shooting creatures on a big screen. In his arms was a long box with a picture of a racing car on the side. "I guess you're really into motorsports, huh?"

"Bring it over here," Claude ordered, gesturing with the pistol.

"Not until you let everyone else in this house go." Braden delivered the words with no emotion, though Marjorie could detect the faintest tremble in his legs where the cloth of his trousers shook. "I've told Felix to phone the police if they're not outside in two minutes." He awkwardly shifted position to check his watch. "Your time's almost gone."

Claude stared. His lips pressed together so

hard they nearly disappeared. On the wall, a clock ticked away the seconds.

One.

Two.

Three.

"Fine." The gunman flicked his eyes around the group while a contemptuous sneer distorted his face. "Get outside."

"I'm not leaving you alone with him," Marjorie protested. "Just dump the box on the ground and come out with us."

"Go!" Claude shouted, pulling back the hammer. "I won't tell you again."

The four of them filed out the back door on unsteady legs. Marjorie tried to keep Braden in her line of sight, but Claude followed them along the hallway and slammed the back door shut.

"You called the police anyway, didn't you?" she asked Felix who was sheltering behind his car. "We need to get them here."

"I called." The man appeared miserable. "When Braden came up the drive, he caught me by surprise. I should be the one in there. I'm the eldest."

"Don't worry about it," Jon said, squeezing the man's shoulder. "We should all focus on getting out of here in one piece."

"How does he have a handgun?" Marjorie asked. "I thought no one had them anymore."

"It looked old." Felix gave a weary shrug. "Maybe it belonged to his father or something. There's a chance it doesn't even work. A lot of those old guns have been disabled so families could keep them as souvenirs."

A second after Felix spoke, a shot rang out, demolishing that hope. The group of five stood there, muscles tensed, not moving.

"Should we go inside?" Marjorie asked, fearing the answer. As she stared at the others, no one said a word. "We could—"

She broke off as tyres crunched on the gravel of the driveway. A police car. Three officers got out, dressed in protective gear from head to toe.

"He's inside," she shouted, pointing to the house. "One gunman and one hostage."

The door opened and three police officers reacted, crouching and aiming rifles at the property. Braden stood in the opening, hands in the air.

"We need an ambulance," he shouted, kicking the pistol outside. "Claude Skinner's been shot."

CHAPTER FIFTEEN

"Wait, wait," Esme said, holding her hand up. "Are you saying a *kitten* shot Claude?"

Marjorie laughed and leaned back in her chair. She'd heard the story already and knew how it ended. Braden's eyes lingered on her face as he took a sip from his cola, then gave her a slow smile that stirred up butterflies in her belly.

"It wasn't *a* kitten," he corrected, turning back to his audience. "It was a pair. Claude had propped the gun on the mantelpiece while he examined the box to see it held what he wanted. While he was crouched down, Toil and Trouble pushed the pistol off the shelf, and it shot him right in the leg."

Esme broke into giggles, the good food and good company of the dinner making her giddy. "Please tell me you got a video of the situation. It's too good to lose forever."

"At the time I was more interested in getting myself out of the place alive than recording the event for posterity." Braden took a Christmas cracker as Allie passed them out from a basket and waggled it at Marjorie. "Are you game?"

"What was in the box?" Esme said, tugging at Braden's hand until he dropped the cracker and turned his attention back to her. "Finish the story. This is the most exciting event I've ever been adjacent to in my life."

"I'm not sure I want to talk about that," Braden said while his mouth pulled down at the corners. "Claude Skinner is a nasty piece of work."

"It was a brass knuckleduster," Marjorie

said when it seemed Esme would burst if someone didn't tell her. "Covered in blood."

"Martin Thorpe's blood?" Jerry guessed while Braden nodded. "He killed him?"

"This is where I need to take a step back," he said, holding his hands up. "Marjorie can take over the story from here."

"Claude Skinner was using Martin Thorpe to launder money from his illegal activities. It's why he pulled back from the rest of his clients. Even while he was doing something against the law, he disengaged from our accounts so if he was caught, we wouldn't be dragged down with him."

"Nobility amongst the swine," Jerry said, shaking his head. "I'm glad I just harass the Inland Revenue directly when I need help with my taxes."

"Some of us need more help than a phone call can sort out." Marjorie pushed her plate back, then promptly picked another piece of stuffing up in her fingers and made it disappear. "When his ex-wife hired a forensic accountant to intervene in the divorce settlement, I think he knew the game was up."

"Which left everyone without their favourite accountant." Esme poked Jerry in the ribs. "Apart from those of us who're too cheap to hire help."

"Before he attacked him," Marjorie continued, "Claude Skinner tried to manipulate Martin into continuing his practice. When he found out the accountant loved a particular breed of kitten, he intervened and brought the cat out from under him."

"But didn't he own the cat?" Esme asked with a frown.

"The breeder sold it to Claude for double the price, then told Martin she was giving it to him for free." It had taken a little cajoling via direct message to get the full truth out of the woman, but the breeder had eventually complied.

"But why?" Jerry drained his glass and poured another iced tea from the pitcher in front of them. "If he ended up with the kitten anyway, why bother with the subterfuge?"

"Because Martin thought the kitten was his, then found out Claude had legal title to him and could take him away at any moment. It must have been devastating." Marjorie's lower lip wobbled at the though. "It'd be like finding out you weren't your son's father."

Jerry looked unconvinced. "Yet he still hit him to death?"

"He hit him, but it didn't cause his death. According to Dr Every, Martin drowned his sorrows in a hip flask of brandy before deciding to fix the spouting his neighbour was always bleating about."

"He fell?" Esme's eyes widened, and she covered her mouth with her hand. "You're kidding?"

Braden tapped a drumbeat out on his belly. "It's the inherent danger of performing your own repairs. That's why you'll never find me up a ladder."

"I thought Felix heard the police say it was

murder?" Esme turned and clicked her fingers to get the man's attention, but he didn't budge.

"He must've got the wrong end of the stick and he's not the only one. Claude would've been beside himself when he heard Martin Thorpe had been found dead," Marjorie said, resisting the urge to yawn. Too much turkey. "Then he found out the box he'd stashed the weapon in had disappeared from the front hallway. I don't know if Lillian genuinely confused the different piles or if she was sick of her husband's behaviour and wanted to cause mischief. Either way, she handed a weapon covered in Claude's fingerprints and Martin's blood to the community centre."

"In response to which, he organised a burglary to steal all the presents so he could get the evidence back." Esme finished the story, shaking her head. "That's cold-blooded for you."

"How about we turn our minds to happier matters?" Braden said, jerking his chin towards the chair where Santa was busy dispensing Christmas gifts. "Don't they look happy?"

The children appeared ecstatic. The ones who'd already received their presents were tearing open the exquisitely wrapped gifts to expose their new toys, while others had gone further and wrangled plastic and twist-ties to work them free. A racing car whizzed towards Marjorie's chair and she lifted her feet so it passed underneath, unimpeded.

"What's going on over there?" Esme asked with open suspicion, pointing a finger towards Woody and Jared who were playing with two very familiar black kittens. "I thought giving animals as Christmas gifts was discouraged."

"Not when they're grown men," Marjorie said, folding her arms and smiling. She tilted her head to one side as Jared collapsed in a fit of giggles. "Well, grown-ish. They've been pestering me for the coolest cats in all Hanmer Springs. Apparently, kittens who can shoot bad guys, even by accident, are a sought-after commodity."

Esme laughed then clapped her hands as a round of volunteers brought out a mountain of desserts. "Did you make all of these?"

"Fresh out of the oven this morning," Marjorie said, holding a hand over her plate so no one could fill it with any more treats. She'd sampled each of her tempting desserts to make sure they tasted the right amount of scrumptious and couldn't imagine eating another bite.

Well, okay. She relented for one of the single-serve baked cookies and cream cheesecakes but apart from that...

Maybe a chocolate chip cookie to keep her energy levels up.

"Isn't it time for you to sit on Santa's knee?" Felix called out to Allie as the last child received their present and ran off to open it.

"What are you talking about?" she asked with the ghost of a smile. "I'm far too old for such things."

"Nobody is ever too old for Santa's lap," Marjorie said, winking at Braden as she stood up and walked around the table to stand next to Felix. Dotty hurried out of the adjoining kitchen to join them, undoing her apron and throwing it onto an empty chair.

"I don't—"

Their volunteer Santa—in actuality Ralph from the Hunting & Fishing store in town—slapped his hands on his knees and uttered a boisterous, "Ho, ho, ho! Have you been good this year?"

Allie blushed, holding her hands up to her face to hide her reddening cheeks. "What have you organised?" she said in a scolding tone. "This day is for the families."

"And for the volunteers," Dotty insisted. She nudged Felix in the ribs. "I've already had my gift this morning but you're overdue for your turn."

With some foster parents and children joining in the urging, Allie let herself be cajoled onto Santa's lap. He pulled a small present from the diminished pile and Marjorie reached over to give Jon a high-five. After all, he'd been the one to select the gift based on his stint working at the community centre.

"You didn't have to," Allie said, beaming with pleasure while she fiddled with the ribbons.

Braden slid his arms around Marjorie, and she leaned back against his chest, enjoying the warmth. His soft breath tickled the side of her neck and gently whooshed against her ear.

This was feeling like the best Christmas ever.

"A watch," Allie said, holding the gift up for the room to see. "How did you know?"

"Because you mention it every couple of minutes," Jon said in a mock grumble. "And if we didn't get you a good one of your own, you'd keep borrowing mine."

The room laughed at the good-natured teasing, then cheered as Allie fastened the leather strap around her wrist.

"Oh!" she cried out, stopping midway. "It's engraved! *To the heart of our community.*"

Tears poured down her cheeks, and the room cheered again while Esme fetched her some tissues. "We don't thank you often enough for how much you do for this town," she said as she passed them across. "But we're all very grateful."

As one of the volunteers stumbled under an armful of dirty plates, Marjorie moved away from the celebration and took half her load. Braden caught on a second later, clearing away another few settings and following her through to the kitchen.

"How's Shadow settling back in at your place?" he asked as they scraped food waste into the bins and rinsed off the plates. "He might've torn up my home a bit, but I miss the company."

Marjorie rolled her eyes. "Monkey Business has declared a full-scale war on the poor wee fellow. Right now, as we speak, he's probably rallying his troops to attack." As Braden laughed, she gave a sigh. "It is funny in theory, but I might need to take Jon up on his offer soon before they have a true falling out. Monkey must be three times his size."

"Poor thing. Being bullied is never nice."

A throat cleared behind them and Marjorie was surprised to see Barney Baxter. The builder stood, obviously nervous, rubbing at the back of his neck with his throat struggling to form words.

"Is there something the matter?" she asked in alarm as tears formed in the man's eyes.

Barney shook his head. "Nah. I just miss my wife and son today. We finished up on the job site yesterday, but not in time for the last bus back to Christchurch, and no one had the room free to give me a lift."

"Oh, that's awful." Marjorie waved a hand towards the hall. "Did you get a plate to eat?"

"Yeah, it's been lovely. A young man's sorted me out with a lift home shortly." Barney pointed to Jon who was juggling at least four balls, much to the delight of the entranced group of children surrounding his feet. "But I wanted to see you before I headed off."

"What about?"

The builder tugged at the loose flap of skin under his throat and tipped his head back and forth. "It's the kitten," he finally burst out. "The ugly one. He kind of grew on me and I wondered if I'd be able to offer him a home."

"Ugly?" Braden said, his nostrils pinching together. "You'd better not be talking about my former cat."

"No offence," Barney said, backing up a step and holding his hand out. "It's just a nickname. Look." He pulled a phone out of his back pocket. "This is my son. With the harelip and cleft palate, he gets called ugly a bunch of times. It doesn't stop him from being a beautiful kid."

The pride that shone out of his voice made a lump form in Marjorie's throat. "You want him to have a funny looking kitten?"

"Yeah. He'd love that little sucker no matter how much of his hair falls out." Barney kissed the screen before tucking his phone away. "Now tell me. Is he available or not?"

"He's available." It was Marjorie's turn to take her phone out. "What's your number and I'll send you a form to complete. The SPCA needs to do a house check to make sure you'll provide a suitable home, then he's yours."

Barney's face fell. "That sounds like a long process."

"It'll be a few days longer because of the holidays," Marjorie said truthfully. "But only a week or two, tops." She smiled and sent a few images along after the form. "There's a few pictures and videos to tide you over until then."

"Problem sorted," Braden said as the builder moved away. "Shadow can have a short visit with Jon, then move on to his new home."

With the plates stacked, they moved back to the doorway and Marjorie stood on tiptoe to see Santa dancing with Allie. Happy tears formed in her eyes as she watched the older woman's face glow with joy.

"Is this a coincidence?" Esme asked, walking over to them. "Or is this good planning on your part?"

"What do you mean?" Marjorie frowned in confusion.

Esme pointed a finger up to the centre of the doorway where a sprig of fake mistletoe hung from the frame.

"Well, I'd hate to break with tradition," Braden said, curling an arm around Marjorie's waist and pulling her close. "So, if the lady doesn't mind…?"

As he pressed his lips against hers, Marjorie decided no. No, she didn't mind at all.

Thank you for taking the time to read Lykoi Larceny.

If you enjoyed it, please consider telling your friends or posting a short review. Word of mouth is an author's best friend and much appreciated.

Thank you, again. Katherine Hayton.

ALSO BY KATHERINE HAYTON

Chartreux Shock (Marjorie's Cozy Kitten Café)

Calico Confusion (Marjorie's Cozy Kitten Café)

Charity Shop Haunted Mysteries – Books 1-3

Miss Hawthorne Sits for a Spell (Charity Shop
Haunted Mystery)

Mr Wilmott Gets Old School (Charity Shop
Haunted Mystery)

Mrs Pettigrew Sees a Ghost (Charity Shop
Haunted Mystery)

A Bed for Suite Dreams (A Hotel Inspector Cozy
Mystery)

A Stay With Reservations (A Hotel Inspector Cozy
Mystery)

A Job of Inn Dependence (A Hotel Inspector Cozy
Mystery)

The Double Dip (Honeybee Cozy Mystery)

The Honey Trap (Honeybee Cozy Mystery)

The Buzz Kill (Honeybee Cozy Mystery)

Tea Shop Cozy Mysteries – Books 1-6

Hibiscus Homicide (Tea Shop Cozy Mystery)

Keeping Mums (Tea Shop Cozy Mystery)

Orange Juiced (Tea Shop Cozy Mystery)

Deathbed of Roses (Tea Shop Cozy Mystery)

Berry Murderous (Tea Shop Cozy Mystery)

Pushing Up Daisies (Tea Shop Cozy Mystery)

Food Bowl Mysteries – Books 1-3

You're Kitten Me (Food Bowl Mysteries)

Cat Red-Handed (Food Bowl Mysteries)

An Impawsible Situation (Food Bowl Mysteries)

The Sweet Baked Mysteries - Books 1-6

Cinnamon and Sinfulness (Sweet Baked Mystery)

Raspberries and Retaliation (Sweet Baked Mystery)

Pumpkin Spice & Poisoning (Sweet Baked Mystery)

Blueberries and Bereavement (Sweet Baked Mystery)

Strawberries and Suffering (Sweet Baked Mystery)

Cupcakes and Conspiracies (Sweet Baked Mystery)

The Only Secret Left to Keep (Detective Ngaire Blakes)

The Second Stage of Grief (Detective Ngaire Blakes)

The Three Deaths of Magdalene Lynton (Detective Ngaire Blakes)

Christchurch Crime Thriller Boxset

Breathe and Release (A Christchurch Crime Thriller)

Skeletal (A Christchurch Crime Thriller)

Found, Near Water (A Christchurch Crime Thriller)